Our Little Florentine Cousin of Long Ago

This edition published 2026
by Living Book Press
Copyright © Living Book Press, 2026

ISBN: 978-1-76183-049-5 (hardcover)
         978-1-76183-044-0 (softcover)

First published in 1929.

A catalogue record for this book is available from the National Library of Australia

Our Little Florentine Cousin of Long Ago

by

Anna Constance Winlow

Filippo

Contents

I

A Secret Errand on the Ponte Vecchio

In the very early morning of the thirteenth day of March, 1478—or as the Florentines would have it, 1477, for they did not reckon their New Year's Day until March twenty-fifth—a handsome boy was standing irresolutely on the Old Bridge of Florence. His curling hair, of a length just to sweep his shoulders, was caught by the breeze and blown first across his face and then to his back. The same breeze parted his dark velvet cloak to show its lining of gay *oricello* silk, a lovely reddish color for which his city was noted, and the sky-blue *sajo* or tunic underneath. The boy shivered a trifle, but still hesitated.

Filippo had reached his destination, and, decidedly, he was afraid.

He had ridden down from the Fiesolan hills at more than his usual reckless speed, and left his horse, as he often did, at the hostel near the San Gallo gate. That was all that had been ordinary. For the rest, he could hardly remember ever having come into Fiorenza (the old Tuscan spelling for Florence) so early. It seemed that the only persons yet stirring were various *contadini* (peasants) who had driven their carts or trudged on foot into the city to sell their produce. They were already fighting for the best places in the Mercato Vecchio, the central and most important market, as Filippo had seen as he passed, and also right here in the smaller market at the head of the bridge he was on.

In fact, he had almost been trodden underfoot by a plunging mule when a small peasant boy had twitched its tail. He had just leaped aside in time when the over-tried animal kicked out and sent flying a whole stall of cheeses, apples, and early spring vegetables. It wasn't a thing like that which could frighten Filippo.

On the contrary, he had turned on the boy in a twinkling and given him so sound a cuff that the latter tumbled headfirst into a basket of parsley and herbs, and in getting up crashed first into a sack of artichokes and then against a pannier of eggs not yet unloaded from another mule. What a confusion! The broken eggs had oozed forth in a stream, the vegetables rolled about, the market folk screamed and gesticulated. Impish children had darted in and out among the stalls and carts, slyly stealing this and that tasty morsel. Donkeys had brayed, babies cried, a dog barked loudly. A crowd of men and women in bright costumes had hemmed in Filippo with threatening faces and doubled fists.

It had never occurred to him to pity the poor mistreated animal that was the cause of all the trouble. No, he simply hadn't been going to let himself be made a fool of by an imp of a ragged boy. He had laughed in the faces of the older contadini, stuck his arms akimbo, and with a kick to a rolling onion at his feet, pushed a way clear for himself to the bridge. Despite angry mutters, no one had ventured to attack him.

Giving a toss of the head and a snap of the fingers back at the market folk, he had thus swaggered on to the narrow passage of the Ponte Vecchio (Old Bridge), lined on either

THE OVER-TIRED ANIMAL KICKED OUT.

side by oddly shaped little houses, most of them with shops on the ground floor. This was the most picturesque of the several bridges spanning the river to Oltr' Arno, the section of the city lying south of the Arno. The morning light was dim, and after the open market square, it seemed positively dark between the buildings. Here Filippo stood, his face paling a little, his hand trembling a bit as he drew together his warm cloak.

After standing for five minutes or more before a certain barred door without, however, touching the knocker, he ran a few steps forward. In its middle, for the space of a house or two, the bridge was open to the river. Filippo leaned on the parapet gazing down at the rushing water, which was high and dangerous at this season. Away from the shelter of the houses, the cold breeze could play with him unopposed, and did so. It caught his cloak and set it to billowing like a flag. Then before he knew it, up went his cap from his head and, whirling in the air, slowly settled on the surface of the Arno.

"Diavolo!" exclaimed Filippo ruefully. He peered down after it, and could make it out near one bank. "Hie there!" he called out. "Hie there!" He had spied some fishermen drawing in their nets. "Hie, get my cap, and here's a *denaro* for you when I come down." He drew a coin from his *scarsella* and held it between thumb and finger.

The fishermen seemed too far off to hear. Just then an unkempt barefooted urchin darted out from under the bridge, threw himself boldly into the river, and swam the short distance to the cap, which he carried in his teeth back to shore. He needed all his limbs not to be carried on by the current.

"Good!" shouted Filippo as he saw the boy struggle up to the bank. "Bring it here, and here's a fine *soldo* for you."

"Like fun!" screamed back the other. "I can get six *soldi* for this easy in the Mercato."

"I'll give you six, you thief. Come up here, or I'll break your bones!"

The boy, dripping with water, moved out of sight. Filippo waited for him to appear on the bridge. He waited long before he realized that the little sinner had preferred to give him the slip and slink away to sell or wear the fine velvet cap elsewhere. A bad Easter to the impudent rascal!

Filippo was very angry. How cold the wind was! He moved back between the shops and looked at one fixedly. It, like all the others, was still shuttered and locked. All were as silent as night. His eye wandered up and down reading the signs; they were mostly those of the incomparable artist-jewelers and goldsmiths for which the bridge was already becoming famed.

Only this one sign, with its strange marks that were neither Latin nor Greek, for Filippo knew both, nor good Tuscan Italian, interested him.

Should he do it after all?

It was not that Filippo did not know what the shop was nor who kept it. The shop was supposed to be that of a pharmacist, but everyone knew, or at least so it was said, that its keeper did many strange things that had nothing to do with the compounding of medicines. Filippo knew the man well enough. He had been in his shop, even, but always in the full light of day and with his father. The man was a client of Filippo's father, who was a prominent notary or family lawyer of Florence; lawyers can't always choose their clients, thought Filippo.

"Hang it!" he murmured to himself, "it's too early. Not a church bell has rung yet. To all purposes it's still night—the devil's own time. Anything could happen inside there. Witchcraft—brrr! Why in goodness's name didn't I stay in bed a while longer?"

But Filippo considered it even earlier than it was. He had idled away quite half an hour on the bridge, and now there came a deep harmonious peal followed by others. The church towers of Florence were calling to prayer.

Almost instantly there was an answering stir throughout the City of Flowers. On either side of Filippo, shutters were thrown open, windows and doors unlocked. The lights before the holy pictures on the fronts of some of the houses seemed to grow dimmer. Tradesmen and their wives came out, hesitated on their doorsills to say an Ave Maria. Soon the narrow but well paved streets and handsome *piazze* or squares were fast filling with color and life.

Should he go inside? This one shop had still remained as dark and quiet as the grave. In a burst of resolution, Filippo seized the metal knocker wrought in the form of a bird's head, and clanged it loudly. There was no answer. His quick temper flaring up, Filippo's cheeks burned. He clanged more loudly still, and gave a kick at the stout oaken door. Fear or no fear, he was not going to be rebuffed.

After a time, in which Filippo kept up a continual clang, clang, clang, a head with a long sharp nose and a white night-cap appeared at an upper window. Bah, Maestro Bartolommeo Piccino was hardly terrifying in this guise.

"Let me in," demanded Filippo. "I want to buy something of you."

"Who is it?"

"Filippo de' Nerli, son of Ser Guido." (Maestro was a Florentine title for doctors, etc.; Ser a title for notaries).

"The son of my esteemed lawyer is always welcome," said Maestro Bartolommeo in an humble manner. "But it might be a little early, just a little early, my excellent young friend."

"Early or not, I want to see you!" Between the loss of his cap and the action of the street boy who found it, with Bartolommeo's unctuous voice and the chill of the March morning, Filippo's patience was quite at an end.

"Certainly, oh, certainly then, certainly, assuredly," agreed the figure at the window with conciliatory haste. "I will be right down, my young friend; do you but have the goodness to wait until I am fittingly gowned."

The head disappeared, the window closed—and Filippo's fear came back. Why was the Maestro so willing to see him? Was it merely on his father's account? He remembered only too clearly all their housekeeper, Monna Nannina, had told him about this man's magic-working. Of course his queer doings might be done only to impose on the ignorant, still… How uncanny that sign was above the door! Filippo recalled the interior of the shop—dark, odd-smelling, filled with mysterious objects hung with cobwebs and covered with dust.

How he wished he were not here! Only his pride held him to the spot.

He gave an involuntary start as the iron-hinged door grated open.

"Welcome. Step in," said the long-nosed man, now clad in a skull-cap and a long black gown. "But how pale you are, my young friend. Surely nothing has happened to that worthy gentleman, your father?"

"No," answered Filippo in a hollow voice, as he followed his questioner inside and heard with a gasp the door shut behind him.

"The cold. Doubtless it's the cold. You must drink a few drops of wine. I shall bring you a glass instantly."

"Oh, I couldn't! I couldn't! I am quite all right, with many thanks!" Filippo saw himself poisoned, bewitched, transformed into some mythical animal. In this new alarm, he took courage to clutch Bartolommeo's arm so that the latter could not leave. The arm felt thin and bony under the wide sleeve.

"I must get this over with," thought Filippo, and forced himself to face the long nose and loose yellow skin of the pharmacist. The shop was lit only by a lantern which had been hung on a hook in the ceiling. The light formed peculiar lines and hollows on the old man's visage and gave an unearthly glint to his deep-set eyes. Even at that he was easier to look at than the room—with its flitting shadows, its heavy odors, its rows of mysterious jars and vials.

In a voice he could not make quite steady, Filippo began. "I don't know whether you'll have what I want, Maestro Bartolommeo. You see I want..."

His voice grew more confident as he described what he desired and what he proposed doing with it. To his considerable relief Piccino laughed. Somehow it made the old fellow more human, that laugh.

"I get what you want, ha, ha, ha," chuckled Bartolommeo. "Boys are still boys, I see. Ha! ha!" He began to recite an adventure of his school days long ago, seating himself as he did so on the edge of his counter.

By degrees Filippo discerned a stool standing near the wall and let himself down upon it. He told the pharmacist something about his teacher and his fellow students. The Maestro replied again with other tales, most exciting ones, of a man who, so Bartolommeo said, had found the Philosopher's Stone and could understand all learning and change brass and iron to purest gold. Nobody could guess how he had managed so well, until one night, puff! he disappeared in a little whiff of smoke, and folks knew then that he had sold his soul to the devil.

"Do you know as much as he did?" questioned Filippo suspiciously.

"No, no, my young friend. I know a little of this and a little of that, it may be, but the devil has never come along with a bargain for my soul."

Filippo found himself beginning to like the pharmacist famously. "Tell me more," he urged. "How much do you really know? People say that you are an alchemist yourself and can change all metals to gold and that you have filled up a whole room with gold already. They say also that you can bring back the dead and concoct charms."

Old Bartolommeo's eyes glowed. "As for charms and magic—" He waved his hand. "Charms and magic are not for a poor man like me, a good son of Holy Church. Enough if I discover the great secret—and by San Giovanni, I believe I have my finger nearly upon it!" He had grown very excited. "Gold! Gold! Oh, for the day when I shall draw my wand out of my retort into which nothing has gone save base metals, and find it capped with gold!"

"And will that be soon?" asked Filippo eagerly, carried away by the other's fervor.

"I work and study on the problem day and night. What do I care about compounding drugs and keeping the common people in awe of me by a little harmless mystery! It will be I, I, Bartolommeo Piccino, who will conquer the secret of transmuting metals!" His voice rose triumphantly, then sank. "*Cristo,* I must succeed! I must!"

Filippo started to ask many questions about the process the alchemist was following, for he knew something himself, from reading, of the ancient practice of alchemy. Doubtless Maestro Bartolommeo would have resented the questions from an older person, but he enjoyed talking quite frankly to this handsome and independent boy. When he thought he had said enough, "Come," he suggested, "and I will show you my workroom."

Filippo followed up a dark and winding stair to an upper room, which, however, was itself lit by two small windows in the roof. To the back was a furnace, now cold. From the ceiling hung various kettles and retorts; a table was cluttered with bottles, pieces of metal, little heaps of loose chemicals, and other things. A Latin manuscript, brown with age, richly bound in leather, was open on a stand. Above it was a stump of a candle, some of the grease of which had fallen on the leaves. In one corner of the room was a large object shrouded by a piece of cloth.

Filippo's active mind was fascinated. Making himself at once at home, he burrowed around, inquiring about everything.

The old alchemist had long ago lost the last trace of his too-humble manner toward the son of that important man,

FILIPPO STARTED BACK WITH A CRY.

the notary Guido de' Nerli. He spoke charmingly as equal to equal, and Filippo quite forgot the long nose, the yellow wrinkled skin, and the bent back. For Filippo was in his element. He was reading off scraps of Latin from the parchment pages, studying each object, prying into every nook.

Chalked on the table was an algebraic formula, and Filippo began to study this intently.

"Stay! stay!" smiled Maestro Bartolommeo, showing his teeth broken by age, "that is getting too close to the knowledge for which I have spent my life. Come, instead, over here and see my manikin—I promise you he won't bite!"

Filippo turned, then started back with a cry. The curtain had been lifted, showing a strange grinning figure, inky black but shining with a dullish glow.

Filippo, backed against the door, began with feverish haste to say an Ave Maria. Bartolommeo laughed. "Tut, tut, it's not alive," he chuckled. "You're only looking at the 'watchman' I've made myself to stand guard over my treasures when I'm out. Just a thing of wood and paint, my friend—but I don't tell that to everyone."

To reassure his visitor, Bartolommeo shook the manikin, then held it up by a horn of its head.

Although Filippo had a lively imagination, he was far from being a coward. Seeing that nothing happened, he forced himself to approach, and finally to touch the puppet.

"It's a treasure, Bartolommeo!" he exclaimed, fear and pleasure mingling in his tone, "How I wish I had my sketching materials with me so that I could draw it... But are you sure it is not—that is—that there's no witchcraft about it?"

II

A Sheep on Two Legs

Beautiful Fiorenza had awakened to a rather sober Friday morning, for it was the last week but one in *Quaresima*, that is, Lent. When Filippo left the alchemist's, the city clocks were pointing to a bit after twelve. This was still pleasantly early, for twelve o'clock Florentine time was only eight A.M. of our time. The Florentines counted each new day as beginning at what is our eight o'clock of the previous evening, which they called twenty-four o'clock; our nine P.M. was one o'clock for them, and so on to their twenty-four o'clock.

Leaving the Ponte Vecchio, Filippo hurried the few steps to the little nearby Church of the Holy Apostles. This church was so old that tradition claimed that it had been founded by the great Emperor Charlemagne himself. After mass, Filippo returned through the fruit and vegetable market at the head of the bridge. His eyes were sparkling with fun. "I have loads of time," he thought, pulling out some of the walnuts Bartolommeo had given him and cracking them in his palm.

The little market was now crowded with purchasers as well as sellers. Filippo saw a group of boys tossing coins under an empty stall. A pretty peasant girl with two long braids of black hair over her gaily colored dress and mantle, moved about like a flower herself, calling out: "Flowers for sale; flowers for holy *Gesu*" (Jesus).

Filippo debated whether or not to buy a bunch of wild anemones and iris to lay before the shrine of his patron saint or of the Holy Madonna, but he forgot the impulse as he noticed that a story-teller had seated himself on one of the stone benches. He tried to catch some of what was being told. The crowd around was laughing so heartily that he could not hear a word. "They don't mind making merry in Passion-tide," thought Filippo. He looked around for the flower girl, and found her gone.

"Oh, well," said Filippo to himself, and was about to turn into a narrow street leading to the middle of town. His way was blocked by a procession of barefoot white-clad pilgrims, bearing a cross and sacred banners. Crossing himself and bending his knee, Filippo turned off to the side in the direction of the Palazzo Vecchio. He was so busy planning how he would use the contents of the little parcel he carried under his cloak, he hardly noticed where he went. He laughed silently. It was splendid. Splendid!

Before he knew it he had come upon the splendid *piazza* or square which was the site of the world-famous Palazzo Pub-blico or Palazzo Vecchio. This was the chief seat of government, the State House of Florence. At the end of the *ringhiera*, the stone platform before the palace, was the majestic stone lion called Marzocco, the emblem of the Florentine Republic. The whole *piazza*, like all of Florence, was full of triumphs of art and architecture.

Filippo had a sudden inspiration. He walked eagerly around the Palace of the People, looking up at its four stories of massive stone, the top story, with its open gallery and battlemented roof, projecting like a crown over the rest. From it, in turn, the strong and beautiful tower of the building rose to a height to overlook the whole city. In the arched belfry at its top could be seen the great bell called "The Cow," which when it rang called all citizens to come together. On hearing it ring they said: *"La Vacca mugghia"* (The Cow moos).

"Magnificent!" exulted Filippo. "This gives me the very subject for my Latin poem!

> "Thou stern and stone-clad guardian of our Freedom!
> Thy tower ever watches o'er our State,
> Lest Treason raise its hydra heads among us
> Or outer foes surprise our open gate.
> "To thee Marzocco's kingly eyes are lifted;
> On thee Fiorenza's Lily lies secure…"

Filippo was scanning the Latin lines as he composed them, his eyes turned up to the coats-of-arms of Florence painted across the Palazzo Vecchio below the projecting top story. There were many of these, each recalling some part of Florentine history. Prominent among them were the white lily on a red field, the red lily on a white field, and the golden lilies on a blue field.—Fiorenza was called the City of the Lily.

> "So long as thy proud vigilance endureth
> That long will our sweet Liberty endure…"

continued Filippo. "It begins rather well," he told himself critically; "must be improved, of course." He smiled. He had just remembered that it was commonly said that the "Republic of Florence "was in truth now ruled by a single man, a man without a title or a crown, but yet the equal of kings, though he signed himself simply: "Lorenzo, Citizen of Florence.""

"San Michele!" Filippo exclaimed nearly aloud, "that gives me a title for a pretty essay in Greek or in Latin as my good teacher pleases: 'What Is the Best Form of Government?' Plenty of opportunity in that for quoting the ancient authors the master is so fond of, Plato, Virgil, Cicero, and all the rest. I'll finish my poem first, though. Let me see.

"Thou art in one a bulwark and a beacon… "
As he thought, Filippo had wandered on to the *serraglio*, where the gentle lions belonging to the city were kept. Since Florence had as one of her symbols a stone lion, she thought it fitting to keep also a big family of live lions. There were altogether about thirty of them in the *serraglio*. Filippo bent down to watch more closely the pretty antics of three half-grown cubs at play. Something gleamed at his feet. He picked it up. It was a ring.

Filippo whistled as he gazed at his hand. It was an exquisite piece of jewelry: a stone cut like a rose and held by two tiny doves. "This is a sad loss for someone," thought Filippo. "It is perhaps a betrothal ring." No one was in sight to whom the object was likely to belong; there seemed nothing to do but put it in his pocket.

The clock on the Palazzo Pubblico tower showed there was still over an hour of waiting before Fra Antonio's sermon would begin in the great Cathedral. Filippo wasn't at all anxious to hear the sermon, but his father had made him promise that he would. This Brother Antonio de Vergiegli was being much praised for his Lenten preaching this year. "It'll all be talk of repenting and so on," mused Filippo uncomfortably. "I wonder why I ever agreed to go!"

Well, there was more than plenty of time yet for a ramble through the beautiful city, with its palaces and towers and churches and gardens all so fresh and smiling in the morning sunshine. No place could be so delightful for a stroll. The streets were narrow, and crisscrossed each other in so many patterns that one was forever coming across spots one did not know. The fronts of the stone houses were full of interest. The knockers of the doors and the projecting iron or bronze holders for torches were graven with figures of animals and flowers. Beside or above the doors were in many cases niches containing images of saints or of the Holy Family, some of them in the beautiful blue and white glazed terra-cotta which the Florentine artist, Luca della Robbia, had invented some years before. Through the gratings of gates could be caught glimpses of gardens with iris-bordered walks, slender cypress trees, and playing fountains.

Every church, big and small—and there were over a hundred in the city—was a treasure-house of art. Filippo could not help lingering a while before each one he passed, thinking of the great masters who had helped to rear and to decorate it. He thought of his own painting studies each time, and wondered whether he would ever do any famous works like these. Some of the churches were in connection with the numerous monasteries and nunneries, set in wide-cloistered gardens, above the walls of which showed the tops of orange and lemon and olive and fig trees and the tendrils of grape vines.

Half as numerous as the churches were the open squares,

almost every one of them with at least a statue or two. Then again Filippo would follow a maze of stone-paved streets, where palaces, as the homes of the important families were called, jostled humble houses, and splendid monuments of architecture and art rose in the midst of little shops. Many of the houses over-hung the street in their upper stories, or were adorned with arcades called *logge*. Filippo even looked with interest at the streets themselves, for he had heard travelers say they were far better than those of most of Europe; not only were they paved and drained, but some of them were even provided with sewers.

But most of all, the colorful, changing crowd caught Filippo's eye. He had stopped before the immense church of Santa Croce, where so many famous Florentines were buried. A throng of worshipers was about the doors, as well as three enterprising beggars and several peddlers loudly crying their wares. There was something suspicious about two of the beggars. They looked on the surface pitiable enough, with their bandages and crutches, but Filippo felt sure that he had surprised a sign and a wink between them. He would have been more ready to feel for them, had he not known that Florence provided very liberally for her poor and unfortunates, who seldom needed to beg.

"Faugh," he said to himself, "these two get six times their share of alms. They push their way over everyone. I pity the third beggar." They had almost knocked the third beggar down.

Filippo resolved on a bit of sport. He approached the two, who were close together now, and held out his closed hands as if to drop a coin in each cup. Then, instead, in a flash he snatched a *quattrino* from each, and ran off with a laugh.

The trick worked. The beggars sprang so swiftly after him that their rags and sticks went flying to all sides. The "cripples" were as spry as goats. "Come back, thief! Halt, villain!" they shouted.

"That I won't—for the good of your souls!" laughed Filippo, dodging this way and that to escape them.

"We'll lambaste your hide for you!" screamed the foremost beggar, a big and stalwart fellow who looked good for his word.

"You will, will you?" taunted Filippo. He turned as he ran, and at the instant the beggar's hand was on him.

"I'll show you!" bellowed the fellow, with a vigorous shake of the captive. Filippo gave a quick wriggle, and was free from his grasp. Alas, his cloak was left behind.

It flashed through Filippo's mind that it was going hard with him to be losing all his clothes on one day. He looked around appealingly at the laughing, bravoing crowd. His look was answered, for in a jiffy his wrap had been recovered, and nearly everyone was joining in the hue and cry to hoot the false beggars from the *piazza*.

Before Filippo joined, he tossed the *denari*, with one of his own, to the third beggar.

He followed the chase only a few steps. In the center of the Piazza Santa Croce some youths had started a game of *calcio*, a play resembling football, and Filippo stayed to watch. It was only a practice game, but the teams were fine and evenly matched, and the ball went sailing through the air for a goal. Filippo shouted enthusiastically. His foot ached to join in, though the players were all nearer twenty than thirteen, his age.

A flock of school-boys, with less time to spare than he, came dashing round the corner of the church and past the spot where he stood. "Halt! Halt!" he called after them. "You're losing your shoes!"

"But not our caps!" came the answer from one. "Why, boys, it's Filippo de' Nerli, Lippo the Lively!" said he, coining the nickname then and there.

"Lippo the Lively's been in a fight:
He's lost his cap, if I am right!"
Look at him, comrades! What a sight he is!"

This was turning the tables, and Filippo darted off to catch the hindmost boy, which he did, and held him fast. "He's a hostage," he cried, and would not let him go till the others all came bounding to the rescue.

"Beg for mercy!" they ordered as they fell on him.

"Never!"

"In that case, meet us this afternoon behind San Marco, and we'll play ball."

"Agreed."

"*Addio*, until then."

They separated, and Filippo made a wide circle to return to the neighborhood of the great cathedral. The tangle of winding streets was more full of life than before. Here were monks in their hooded robes, there a sister, yonder a priest. Filippo diverted himself by deciding, from the slight differences in their dress, where the many foreigners he met were from: whether from Rome, or Naples, or Venice, or Milan. He was so absorbed in debating the nationality of two brilliantly clothed young men in parti-colored hose, he tumbled flat over the rope stretched across his path—as was intended he should. Mocking peals of laughter came from above him; the street urchins responsible had wisely perched themselves at the top of an outdoor staircase to an upper floor. Filippo made a start to "rush" them, when—thud! clap! bang!—down came a shower of stones. Ignominy! He had to retreat.

But retreat's not defeat. Filippo only retired to where he could peep out unseen, to wait until his antagonists were off guard. Now's his chance! He was on them like a whirlwind, and born fighters though the street boys were, it's doubtful that they got the best of it! Filippo knocked their heads together, "To show you not to meddle again!" and passed on without a backward glance.

He was quite put out by this last adventure, "To have to fight little ruffians like that!" and especially when he recognized Pietro Tosa, the cloth merchant, standing in front of his rich shop, and thought he detected a smile as the merchant greeted him. "I suppose I do look disreputable after all this, but *Santa Maria!* can I help it?" he said to himself.

He regained his spirits after a moment, however, and continued calling out to the young apprentices who hurried by, "Whither so fast?" and to those that loitered on their errands to play, sarcastically, "There's plenty of time in the world, I see!"

In this way he wandered around to the streets mainly inhabited by the wool industry. He saw the headquarters of the *Arte delta Lana* (Wool Association), opposite the Church of Our San Michele, and its sign of two lambs. Practically every citizen of Florence, no matter what his occupation, belonged to one of the associations called *arti*, or guilds, which regulated everything concerning their own crafts or professions. Filippo's father belonged of course to the guild of notaries and judges; his uncle was a member of the Wool Guild.

Filippo was just now passing the prosperous *bottega* of this uncle. He noticed a lively, laughing knot of young apprentices gathered about the door. He caught some of their exclamations: "Ba, I don't believe it is a sheep!" "Oh, it is! it is!" "Santa Maria protect us!" "Give a pull at its wool!"

Then he himself was spied. "It is the nephew of *il padrone*" (the master). "Excellent! Call him over." "Hie, Filippo, come hither; we've something to show you."

Filippo sauntered across the street, well on guard for some good-natured joke from the merry fellows. They formed a ring about him as they conducted him into the workshop. In the first room were great piles of finely spun wool, steaming vats of dye on the brick stove, lines of newly colored cloth and hanks of yarn. Two young workers were each engaged at a small loom, while other youths were busy watching the vats and lifting out the wool to dry. However, they all, weavers and dyers, left their work with alacrity to follow into the long inner room. This was the room of the skilled craftsmen.

Here, along the entire length of opposite walls, were very large looms, with half completed pieces of two varieties of the magnificent cloths for which Florence was world-famous, splendidly figured and colored. The designs seemed fit for kings' robes. The weavers here, too, some of them middle-aged men, smiled, and greeted Filippo. The gray-haired foreman, coming forward with a paper on which he was sketching out a pattern of lions and lilies said, "Welcome."

The apprentices pulled Filippo on into a third room, which opened on a courtyard.

"Bring the creature in, Corso. We have a visitor."

A mischievous, black-eyed lad thrust his head, tousled with bits of wool, in the back door and said gravely: "The animal's getting contrary, my friends. I'll have to have some help."

Several of the boys hurried to his aid, some shuffling and giggling were heard, and after a few moments the voice of the tousled lad called out: "Now, Messer Filippo, you shall see a phenomenon!"

The boys re-entered, flushed and panting, dragging and pushing an upright woolly animal whose front feet hung in the manner of a kangaroo's. The creature was keeping its captors on the jump by butting its horned head at them, first this way, then that, like a young goat. The tousled boy pulled it to the middle of the room, brought it to a standstill with a dexterous twist of the rope, dodged a thrust of the beast's head, and gave an appreciative click of his tongue at the effect.

"Observe!" he panted to Filippo. "Was the like ever seen? An upright sheep it is, *per Bacco!* I wager there's not another such in any land in Italy!"

"I agree with you," nodded Filippo, "except for the word 'another.'"

"What do you mean?" retorted the other in a hurt tone. "Here's the beast before you."

At this, the creature in question emitted a long, melancholy "Baa-as-aa."

"Ah-ho," said Filippo, outwardly falling in with the jest, and inwardly smiling at an idea which occurred to him, "and where did you get this miraculous animal? But—but—are you sure it is not—" he pretended to draw back in affright, "not—the Evil One himself?"

Some of the young apprentices of twelve and fourteen looked really scared at this supposition, and shrank behind their elders. The young weavers of eighteen and twenty, however, only laughed. A chorus of voices hastened to tell Filippo: "Oh, Corso here brought it in this morning from the country. It's a yearling. It was born last spring at a twin birth with a perfectly ordinary lamb. The ewe, its mother, Corso's grandfather said, was so ashamed of it that she did nothing except bite it, so he gave it to Corso for a present."

"Yes," added Corso himself, "and I expect to make my fortune with it. I'm sure Lorenzo de' Medici will be glad to buy it."

"That's a brilliant idea," pronounced Filippo heartily. "I'm certain Lorenzo it Magnifico will be charmed with the creature. Only—" He affected to hesitate. "Only, if there should be any devilry about it, and Lorenzo should come to harm, it would be just like having murder and treason on your soul. You must make sure first."

"How?" asked Corso, uncomfortably.

"Yes, how? But how?" echoed gay and excited voices.

"In this way," said Filippo very gravely. "I have read in a book of magic that the devil hates the color red, the color of Our Lord's wounds. Now I see yonder a vat of scarlet dye that hasn't been heated today. We will just dip this animal in it. If it remains a sheep, well and good. If, on the contrary, there's anything unnatural, we'll soon see!"

No sooner said than done! The boys seized on the supposed sheep, whose struggles seemed much more genuine now than before, and hauled it, kicking, to the vat. The older weavers laughed loudly from their posts in the door-way. The apprentices took firmer grips on the beast, and—despite squirms, kicks, and blows—raised it over the extra vat of dye.

"Oh! Oh! Oh!" wailed a smothered voice. "Don't dip me! Don't! Let me out!"

The young men, roaring with merriment, yelled from the door: "Give him a sousing. Plunge him in! Don't let him off!"

At this, with a frantic lurch and a scream of terror, the sheep wrenched free. Its head fell off, its body ripped open—and there was a youngster somewhat under Filippo's age!

"Bravo!" cried Filippo. "Did I not say my test would be a revelation! Here we have the yearling lamb, the twin of a sheep, and all the rest of it—without the wool!"

"Whew, it was hot," gasped the ex-sheep, wiping his red and streaming face.

"Never you mind," said the lad with the tousled hair, putting his arm around him. "You did your part splendidly, Jacopo."

"That you did," said Filippo, holding out his hands to both. "But where did you get the wonderful costume? I have never seen so fine a disguise."

"Ah, there's the point," returned Corso, for Jacopo was nearly too exhausted to answer. "That's a costume that's going to be used in the *festa* of San Giovanni this year. And no wonder it's fine! You could never guess who made it!"

"Some great artist, no doubt; for they nearly all turn their hands occasionally to designing masquerades for our great holidays."

"Not a great artist yet. 'Tis by a pupil of Cosimo Rosselli—a mere youth—but the master says he will be famous some day."

"Ah, yes!" said Filippo, his eyes sparkling with interest. "Look at that head and face! How natural they are, yet there's something half human about the expression, too. It makes me think of a faun. There's the touch of a genius there… What does this young artist call himself?"

"He goes by name of Piero di Cosimo. I'm related to him," confessed Corso, beaming with pride. "That's why he loaned me the costume. He's made it for the Wool Guild to use in the great *festa* procession."

"That's why I was so afraid you'd dip me in the red dye!" put in Jacopo. "Wouldn't a red sheep look funny?—and Piero and Corso and I'd have all got into such trouble!"

"And now, lads, back to work," called the kindly foreman, with his eyes still twinkling at the end of the jest. And to Filippo: "You've a ready wit, boy; I'm afraid if you had set your heart on learning the trade of weaving with us, you'd make our *bottega* even more lively than it is."

The apprentices trooped through the rooms to see their visitor off, while the men twitted them pleasantly and congratulated both Jacopo and Corso, and Filippo. The latter left amid a shower of *"addios"* and "come again."

III

Filippo Serves a Damsel

*A*t the first street turning after leaving the weaving shop, Filippo came face to face with a tall, important-looking man, clad in a long flowing garment of fine dark cloth, called a *lucco*. Unpleasant encounter!

"What! you here, Filippo? This is the second time in a week that you've absented yourself from study without leave! For what do you think I am paying one of the best masters of Florence to instruct you with my own children?"

"Father told me to hear Fra Antonio preach at Il Duomo" (the Cathedral) "before coming to your house. I am waiting until it's time."

"Time!" echoed Filippo's uncle, growing red in the face. "It's an hour after the time for his sermon!"

"But that's impossible, Uncle Domenico," returned Filippo in an honestly bewildered tone. "It's not quite fourteen yet. Look at that clock. I'll be at the cathedral in a jiffy."

"Fourteen! Fourteen! Who's talking of fourteen? Brother Antonio has been preaching at *thirteen* o'clock all this week."

"He has? *Cristo*, I didn't know it."

"You'll have to wait until his next sermon, which is at fifteen, if you are to hear him today. But I hope you will spend the interval in a useful manner."

"Certainly, uncle," replied Filippo demurely. "I am composing a pretty Latin poem on Florentine liberty, and planning an essay on the art of government. You must listen to the poem… It's not quite finished."

"Ah, boy, boy, you could be as great a marvel of learning as Angelo Poliziano if you would only apply yourself!" The uncle's face had softened into tender pride as his nephew recited the poem, which now numbered over fifty lines. He put his arm around Filippo.

Filippo did not escape without hearing a rather lengthy lecture on making the most of the shining hours of his youth, ending with: "Well, run along, you scamp, and good luck to you."

"Uncle's a little tiresome, like my cousins—except Margherita," he thought, as he turned into the very large market square called Mercato Vecchio (Old Market). Of all colorful spots in colorful Florence, this seemed the most colorful. Every native of the city and countryside seemed here to be jostled in the narrow ways between the stalls. This was the famous center of Florence. Thrifty matrons and pretty servant girls were abroad with baskets for the morning's shopping. Wealthy ladies were stopping on their way from church, at the shops that lined the *piazza*, to order this and that adornment they wanted ready for Easter. *Contadini*, country men and women, were at the stalls. Rich merchants and bankers, renowned artists and sculptors, authors, members of the government, travelers on horseback, churchmen, thieves, street boys, monks, sisters of charity, weavers, goldsmiths, dyers, jewelers, the young, the old, the rich and the poor, everyone that made up the life of the city, was bound at one time or another to be seen.

As if in proof that absolutely everybody could be found here, Filippo suddenly gave an exclamation of recognition and ran to a sturdy country woman in a red hood and green gown. "Nannina! Why what on earth are you doing down here in the city?"

"Buying things for Easter, to be sure, young master. You wouldn't want the day to go by without a new thing in the house, would you?"

"Of course not, Monna Nannina," laughed Filippo, slipping his arm through the handle of the basket she carried and preparing to open the lid.

"Oh, no, you don't!" said Monna Nannina, likewise laughing, but holding fast the lid. "They're surprises—secrets. You'll know what's in here in good time."

"Ah, Monna Nannina, do show me, do!" coaxed Filippo. "Just a little bit of a peep, just the tiniest one." Then, seeing that Nannina only shook her head: "I have a secret, too, Nannina. Just guess! If you'll show me yours, I'll show you mine."

Nannina was at once tingling with curiosity. "I don't believe you," she began by way of yielding. "But if you have an honest-to-goodness package there, you may look at mine."

The cover was off in no time, and Filippo gaily stuck out his tongue as if to lick up all the delicacies in the basket, which promised fine cakes and sweets for Easter Sunday.

"And now," said Nannina eagerly, "show me what you have, Filippo."

"That wasn't agreed: you only said if I *did* have a package, I might look at yours."

"You mischievous mouse!" exclaimed Nannina, giving a playful pull to his hair. "And you've left your cap behind somewhere, too."

Filippo wriggled loose and added: "But I'll show my secret to you. Here it is." He took out a little packet, opened it, and disclosed a handful of red powder.

"Oh, is that all!" murmured the house-keeper in disappointment. "But what is it, Filippo? Is it paint powder?"

"Not on your life. It's magic," said Filippo mystifyingly. "I'm going to cause a miracle with it… Here, Nannina, I'll give you this red apple and you give me some of those pine-nuts you have."

"All right." Monna Nannina took the apple and began to munch it, after pouring into the boy's *scarsella*, or hanging purse, a small handful of the little nuts. "But, Filippo, come with me into this shop; where did you get that queer powder? Of course I know you're fooling about its being magic?" There was a trace of a question in the last sentence.

"Well, Monna," answered Filippo, accompanying her inside, "it may be magic and it may not—as you please. It's from Maestro Bartolommeo Piccino."

The effect of a thunderclap could not have been greater. "From that man!" screamed the superstitious peasant woman. "That wizard!"

"You're eating one of his apples," said Filippo teasingly.

With a cry of profound terror, the peasant woman rushed screaming from the shop, flinging the apple away from her as if it had been poisoned. Filippo dashed after her. "Stop, stop, Nannina! The apple wasn't from Bartolommeo. Forgive me. By all the Saints and may I be stricken dead it wasn't. I got nothing to eat from him but some walnuts. Oh, forgive me, Nannina!"

Filippo had at last caught up with her. "Swear it to me," she said. "Oh, oh, oh! I feel odd inside already."

It took the most solemn oaths to convince the poor woman of the truth of the matter, and hardly had her face cleared, than she was filled with a new alarm. "Oh, Filippo, oh, my pigeon, my baby, have you eaten any of the walnuts?"

"I—I—" He hated to frighten her again.

"Oh, holy Mother! You have! You have!" Monna Nannina buried her head in her apron. From out the cloth came moans of: "Oh, oh, you'll change into some animal. You'll grow a tail. Oh, oh, oh. My poor little Philip, my Filippino, my little master."

"Come, come, Monna Nannina," chided Filippo, putting his arm around her protectingly. "I'm just the same as ever, am I not? I ate the nuts over an hour ago. Why should old Bartolommeo want to bewitch me, of all persons? Father's done him many favors."

"Yes, yes, that's so," acknowledged the housekeeper, raising her head. "Oh, Filippino, thou art such a good boy, and to think of thy mortal danger! But promise me, Filippo, that you won't eat any more of that demon's nuts."

She was quite comforted by the time that she, accompanied by Filippo, had finished her purchases in the Mercato. He walked with her half way to the San Gallo Gate, but at the Monastery of San Marco he had to turn back to reach his own destination in time.

However, when he returned to the Piazza del Duomo, close to the Mercato Vecchio, he had still a few minutes to spare. Here were what were perhaps the three most famous buildings of all the famous buildings of Florence: the great Cathedral of Santa Maria del Fiore, the fourth largest church in Europe; its *campanile* or bell-tower, standing beside it; and opposite, the most ancient church in the city, San Giovanni, where Filippo, like every child born in Florence, had been baptized when a baby.

Standing at the edge of the *piazza*, Filippo lost himself in delight in gazing at the huge dome and colored-marble walls of the magnificent cathedral, and in letting his eyes travel up and up Giotto's towering Campanile, its slender beauty making him catch his breath. He went closer, as he had done hundreds of times before, to study the many sculptured pictures with which the whole lower part of the tower was adorned. "What a master Giotto was!" he thought. "Surely there will never be another belfry on earth to compare with this one he designed when he was nearly seventy years old; and he started life as a poor peasant boy who drew, on stones, pictures of his father's sheep."

There was no time to pass over to the eight-sided Church of San Giovanni Battista, St. John the Baptist, so old that some people said that it was built out of the ruins of a pagan temple to Mars, although, as always, Filippo longed to stand before the world-renowned doors made by Lorenzo Ghiberti, with the Bible stories they told in bronze. Instead, he followed the crowd into the dim, majestic interior of the great cathedral.

When he came out, he did not look altogether happy. As he had anticipated, the preaching had been of repentance and atonement. He began to wonder whether the joke he proposed playing with his red powder was not wicked, particularly at this time of Lenten penitence. He felt tempted, as he neared the river once more, to toss the little parcel away. "Yet it was so much trouble to get," he mused regretfully. "First, there was getting up so early; second, riding down from Fiesole before daybreak—I might have broken my neck or been robbed; third, the trouble of awaking the inn-keeper so he would care for my horse; fourth, the loss of my cap; fifth—let me see; well, I really was rather afraid to go into old Bartolommeo's house. After all, there are very peculiar tales told about him. I wonder whether that black manikin of his was not a warning to me?"

Thinking thus, and also feeling very hungry, for he was somewhat late for comestio, the first meal of the day, which he generally ate with his cousins at fifteen o'clock (eleven), Filippo skirted the river to the Bridge of the Holy Trinity, to cross over to Oltr' Arno, where his uncle lived near the fine, but unfinished, church of Santo Spirito. As he walked along, his attention was attracted by the conduct of two women walking in front of him. One of them, clothed in a *giornee* or over-dress of brocaded silk, seemed from the back a young maiden. Her companion, who was plainly much older, was in a red mantle, and was carrying the wrap of the other. Instead of walking with the usual graceful and proud carriage of Florentine ladies, they were bent as if looking for something.

They moved so slowly, that Filippo was in a moment close enough to hear the elder say: "In my opinion, it is perfectly useless looking further, Madonna. Someone has picked it up."

At these words, the maiden, half turning around, threw up her head in a despairing gesture, so that her scarf fell from her flowing curls, and then she sank down right upon the flagstones. "Monna Gemma, Monna Gemma," Filippo heard her sob, "whatever shall I do? It was all that I had to remember him by until he comes back from the East."

"Let me serve you, Madonna," said Filippo suddenly, "I will hunt all day for whatever you have lost!"

The damsel started, then slowly raised her wet face with a faint sad smile at the boy's offer. She was very beautiful.

"I am afraid it is too late for a knight in this case," she said gently. "It is very weak of me to have given way to my feelings like this, but—but it meant so much to me. I thank you from my heart, dear lad, for your offer, none the less." She touched his arm with her slender hand to steady herself as she rose to her feet.

"But will you not at least tell me what you have lost, Bella Donna?" asked Filippo. Under his breath he added: "And I will find it if it is above ground!"

"It was—it was a ring wrought with two doves and a rose."

"Madonna! Madonna!" cried Filippo joyously, dropping to one knee. "It is here! I have it!" He drew out the ring he had found by the enclosure of the lions, and laid it in her hand.

With a little cry of joy, the maiden seized on and kissed her new knight's hand, then pressed the ring to her lips again and again. "How can I thank you!" she exclaimed. She reached towards her purse, then blushed anew at the hurt expression on Filippo's proud face.

"Forgive me," she murmured. "Ah," she said, "you are too young to know all this ring means to me! It is my one, my precious gift from my beloved until he comes back to Florence. I tell you this so you may know the inestimable service

HE DREW OUT THE RING AND LAID IT IN HER HAND.

you have done me, Bianca Roselli. Tell me your name, too, that we may remember each other as friends."

"We had searched all the morning; we are sinking with fatigue," put in the red-mantled dame, taking the maiden's arm.

"I shall remember you in my thoughts and in my prayers, Filippo," called back the damsel.

Filippo left them with his head in the clouds, where he was already improvising a song to La Bella Bianca on his lute:

"She is a lily in her grace!
'Tis my delight to serve her.
The white rose envies her her face!
Can any man deserve her?"

He had reached the middle of the Ponte Santa Trinita, hearing still in imagination the sweet music of his instrument accompanying his song, when he was startled by a scream of terror almost directly below him. Leaping to the parapet, he instantly took in the cause.

A small boy, of perhaps eight years, was clinging desperately to an overturned boat. It was plain that his little hands could withstand the current hardly a moment longer.

IV

The Fight for Life, and After

Hesitating not a second, Filippo set his hand to the parapet, vaulted up, and threw himself headlong into the rushing tide.

Down, down he went, with a great roaring in his ears; and then more slowly upward. His muscles, trained and hardened though they were by fencing, riding, tilting, and swimming, were almost powerless here. He was swept onward even as he rose to the surface, opening his eyes in a wild stare to see where his goal lay.

By a great blessing Filippo landed east of his object, so that he did not have to breast the current. But the boat, too, was being borne on to the west, with the child clinging to it. Yet, being a big object, it was moving slowly, and Filippo was making almost directly for it.

But would there be time? The child cried out again, and for an instant Filippo thought he had loosened his hold.

With all the strength that was in him, Filippo swerved into line with the skiff and swam forward with the tide.

A violent shock! He had hit the upturned boat.

But—too late!—the boy was gone. Automatically drawing in a deep breath, Filippo let go, and dived.

Almost before he had opened his eyes under water, he felt

an object, a leg, an arm. Slowly, slowly, with great effort, he rose to the surface, dragging the other with him.

Where were they? Where was the boat? Could they reach it?

The little boy had clutched his rescuer around the neck. "Let loose! Let loose! Hold my clothes!" came from Filippo in gurgling gasps. The child was game, and despite his wild terror, did so.

Then, with this great weight impeding him, Filippo swam on, hardly able now to keep afloat. His head went so low that he could scarcely breathe. He would throw back his neck so as to get a whiff of air, then seem to sink, lower… still lower.

There was an awful throbbing in his temples. He could hardly see. Where… was… the… boat…?

There seemed to be many sounds… shouting… screaming. This must be the end.

What was this great weight dragging at him? He must shake himself. No, no; it was the child. Oh, the great tumult in his ears, like the roaring of cataracts filled with human voices.

Was the child loosening his hold? He must save him… Must save him… Grasp him with one hand.

Down… down… down…

All was over.

Filippo came quickly to himself, to find that he was lying on the northern bank just west of the Ponte alla Carraja. A considerable crowd, some of them wet and dripping, others with ropes and planks, were about him. "You only swallowed a cup or two of river water," said a rough artisan, in a leather jerkin and a coat of coarse wool, cheerfully. "You'll be all right in no time."

Filippo lay for a moment too exhausted to think, then suddenly sat up with an excited question: "Where is the boy?"

Hardly had he spoken than he felt arms around his neck and a child's face pressed against his hair. The younger boy, kept on top by his rescuer, had been scarcely affected at all.

Coming around now to the front, he commanded with youthful authority: "Bring him to my palace. I'm Virginio Pazzi."

He mentioned the not far distant home of one branch of this important family. The crowd good-heartedly insisted on making a handseat for Filippo, although he protested that he was quite recovered. "Make way! Make way for the David!" shouted the crowd, swinging along at a lively gait and making a little festival out of the occasion. The artisan in the leather jerkin swung Virginio up to one shoulder and formed one flank. A young man in black doublet and three-colored hose waved his cap.

In this way Filippo found himself within a very short time before one of the smaller of the Pazzi palaces, made of great blocks of stone like the usual Florentine palazzo. Virginio led him into a room with little furniture, but sumptuously decorated with paintings, sculpture, and magnificent hangings and displays of gold and silver. Ordering a servant to make a rousing fire in the great fireplace, he conducted Filippo on to his own bedroom, with its bed hung with brocaded tapestries, where both boys stripped off their dripping garments.

"I'm afraid you'll look very funny in my clothes," said Virginio, laughing. "Well, no matter; I'll tell the servants to dry yours as quickly as possible. I'm home alone today," he went on. "My tutor was called away." Then suddenly interrupting himself: "Santa Maria, what do I not owe to you! You saved me in the very nick of time; I couldn't hold on any longer. I shall love you always."

"It was nothing," returned Filippo. "I think I did rather badly. I'm ashamed I didn't swim better than I did."

"Ashamed! The men who pulled us in were all saying that they would never have ventured to do what you did—to jump down from the bridge into the middle of the river when it's swollen as it is now."

"But how did you come to be out in it, Virginio?"

"The little boat was tied to shore—the rope was nice and long, so I thought I'd pull it up, climb in, and try paddling around a bit. It was fine sport, only suddenly I noticed the rope had broken loose. I was frightened lest I couldn't paddle back to shore, leaped up—and the boat overturned."

As the boys talked, they had returned to the first room, where they settled themselves on the seats inside the enormous fireplace, on the hearth of which the flames now crackled and danced.

"But what is your name?" asked Virginio.

"Filippo de' Nerli."

"Ah, I know: the son of Ser Guido. I'm grateful to you forever. If Virginio Pazzi can ever do anything for you—" said the young boy very seriously.

Filippo laughed, and took his hand. "You can do something right now," he smiled. "Have some food brought here where it is warm. I have missed comestio today."

Virginio clapped his hands with pleasure, and they were soon eating bowls of hot soup made from vegetable stock poured over bread soaked in olive oil; after this came more substantial fare, finished off with some delicious sweetmeats made of sugar and almonds and pine-nuts.

"Yes," said little Virginio, following up his idea, "I am a Pazzi and I may some day be able to serve you. Ours is a very important family; and it is going to be more important," he added, and paused mysteriously.

"Is it?" said Filippo, rather amused by the boy.

"Ah, yes. I have heard. They don't know it, but I have listened at the doors. They are going to kill Lorenzo de' Medici and his brother, and then we will rule Florence instead of him."

Filippo jumped up with a startled and shocked face. "What! Surely your father isn't—"

Virginio was not old enough to grasp the impression he was making. "Why, no," he replied rather regretfully, "papa won't have anything to do with it; I don't know why: Lorenzo de' Medici has done many things against our House."

"But—why, it isn't possible that anyone would think of killing him! How do you know?"

The little boy was delighted that he seemed to be interesting Filippo. "I tell you I heard it all. Papa took me only yesterday to the palace of Francesco Pazzi, who has come back from Rome. Then we rode out to Montughi, and they thought I was playing in the garden, but I listened at the door and peeped through the crack. There was a lot of foreigners there with the men of our family, and Francesco talked to them. He said: 'We will have help from other states who are enemies of Florence, and we will rouse the people, and we will be swept into power in the place of the Medici.' And he said right out: 'Lorenzo and Giuliano de' Medici must be killed,' and nearly everyone agreed, but papa said: 'It is wrong; I will have nothing to do with it.'"

"San Michele!" exclaimed Filippo, his face white, "when and how will this"—he was about to say, "wicked," and stopped—"this—deed be done?"

"Oh, they could not decide; some were saying one thing and some another, until I got tired of listening."

So it was only something talked of! That might mean nothing at all. Filippo felt considerably relieved. None the less, he tried to find out more, but Virginio had told him all he knew. The latter proposed, as Filippo's clothes were now dry, that he dress and come out into the garden.

Going to study had quite slipped Filippo's mind, and he assented readily. Together they wandered under the oranges and cypresses and rose vines, plucking a violet here and there to twist into a flower wreath, and looking at the statues set among the shrubbery. Then Filippo made Virginio radiant with delight by telling him to bring out foils and he would play at fencing with him.

The art of swordsmanship was just beginning to be finely developed, but Filippo was having instruction thrice a week from the best Florentine masters, and already was a graceful fencer for the time. Virginio watched in admiration as his guest illustrated different thrusts with the blunted rapier, and parries with the wooden practice dagger. Then Filippo watched Virginio go through his exercises, and showed him how to improve this 'and that thrust, and shift and recover his body with the lightning speed necessary in rapier play.

"The whole matter is, in making a hit, not to leave yourself open to be hit in turn," laughed Filippo, passing his sword at an imaginary antagonist, and protecting his own body by the movement of the dagger in his left hand.

In this way time passed quickly, and it was past mid-afternoon when Filippo said good-by. Far from feeling tired by the adventures of the day, he was as full of lively energy as usual. He walked briskly the mile or so to the great monastery of San Marco, one of the largest in Italy. Here in the church and cloisters were many of the paintings of the good Friar Angelico, among the most appealing in Christian art, and many relics of Saint Antonino, who had been prior of this monastery before becoming Archbishop of Florence, in which latter high post he had continued his life of charity and self-denial for fifteen years. Although he had now been dead seventeen years, people still reverently remembered his good works and how he had lived in the barest poverty, spending all his vast income for the poor.

Behind San Marco, and extending hence to the city wall, was a splendid open space where Florentine boys and men were usually at play. Here, to one side, was a court for playing the graceful ball game of *pallone*. Some youths were hot at it, hitting the good-sized ball from fist to fist, trying to prevent its coming to rest on their side of the field.

Filippo, however, after glancing at them, found himself more interested in some younger boys, who were engaged in the game called *pome* or *apple*. An apple was hanging on a string from a spreading branch of a tree, at a distance of about five feet from the ground. Three lads were taking turns at running at it full tilt, and when within a certain distance, throwing a dart in an effort to pierce the fruit.

This was very far from an easy matter. So far, none of the

three had been successful, though one of the boys had three times thrown his weapon so that it grazed the apple and set it to swaying violently.

"Bravo!" cried Filippo at the last time the dart brushed the difficult target. "I will stake on you! Win, comrade, win!"

The best player, a boy as handsome as Filippo but with light colored hair in place of Filippo's dark, turned half around with a smile and nod. "There's something very familiar about that boy," thought Filippo at once. He wrinkled his brow in trying to place him.

It had come the turn of Filippo's champion again. With a smiling glance at Filippo, he balanced his missile, looked keenly at the target, and sped off as lightly as the breeze. As he neared the apple, he seemed to poise even as he ran. His dart flashed like a lightning streak. The dart had split the apple.

For a second it hung there quivering, then apple and dart fell together to the ground, the former separating into two halves as cleanly cut as by a knife.

"It was agreed that we should have five turns each, and Rinaldo here and I have had only four," said one of the other two boys, not too graciously.

"Certainly," returned the winner, and going to his coat, which he had flung off on the grass, he brought another apple. It was suspended as the first had been. Rinaldo prepared to take his turn.

He ran and threw well, but far from perfectly. Then it was the chance of the boy who had demanded his fifth turn to prove himself.

He took his position with far more deliberation than had Rinaldo, flexed his muscles, tried a second way of grasping his dart, and at last ran, but not as fast as he might have. His dart whizzed through the air, not near enough to make the apple give even a quiver.

"Per Bacco!" cried Filippo, "you are pretty players, all of you!—only one of you able to hit the target once out of your fifteen throws! I give an apple's worth of credit to the victor, and that is all."

"It is easy to be a hero when one is not in the combat," retorted the boy who had split the apple, coming to the defense of himself and his companions.

"I expect no more of others than I can do myself!" flashed back Filippo, coloring at the implication of the other's remark.

"Ah, so! If your arm is as brilliant as your tongue, you are very welcome to join in our game."

"That is no more than my right, after what you just said!" Filippo was already throwing off his cloak.

"Come, Rinaldo," said the other boy sourly, "'tis nearly time for *prandium*" (the evening meal). With a curt nod he moved off. Rinaldo hesitated, said he thought he'd better be going, and hurried after his comrade.

"Well," said the first boy, looking at Filippo, "the contest is up to us now."

"Exactly. Three strikes win the game."

"Agreed. But you have not your own dart. Will you try this one of mine first? I am pretty well 'warmed up' to it now."

Filippo shook his head. "Thank you; it is not necessary."

The other indicated for Filippo to be first, and Filippo, feeling himself the injured party, accepted the slight advantage in being first. The apple circled tantalizingly in the faint breeze.

Filippo ran and threw. His dart brushed the apple, but no more.

The other let his dart fly.

"You have hit!" cried Filippo, as the missile fell to the ground.

"No, just grazed it."

"No, no. I saw the dart pierce the apple." Filippo ran to the target, and found as he had expected a chunk of it upon the earth beneath. "First hit," he said, returning to his place.

He ran again; and a second time, by as small a margin, missed.

The other took his second turn, and also missed by a hairsbreadth.

Filippo tried for a third time, sending the dart with the beautiful grace that characterized all his movements.

"You have struck," said his adversary.

"You are mistaken," returned Filippo. "It touched the apple but did not pierce it."

The two walked together to look at the target. There was a rent along one side made by the sharp point of the weapon.

"It doesn't count," said Filippo.

"It certainly does."

"It does not. I have never needed to win by half-way strokes."

"In that case, my hit does not count either," returned the fair-haired boy. "It did not bring down the apple."

After some protest from Filippo, they set-to again on an even basis. The stranger brought down the prize with his first throw. Filippo tried his luck on a new apple, and chipped it. After this, there were several throws on both sides that were close but not conclusive. Filippo tried again, and knocked a big piece from the apple.

Some indifferent plays followed. Probably because he was in truth quite tired, Filippo was hardly improving his throws. For the third time that day, the stranger brought down the *pome.*

"You have won," said Filippo, his face rather pale, but no quaver in his sweet ringing voice.

"Not so." The other threw again, and as luck would have it, sent the apple once more to earth. "Well," he smiled, "you are a fair player, friend, but not up to your boasting."

Filippo's cheeks burned red. He looked at the other silently. He could not bring himself to make excuses, though he knew inwardly that he had been very foolish to engage in this contest on the same day that he had been so taxed by the courageous river rescue that he had fainted.

Of this, of course, the other knew nothing. Although generous and courteous by nature, he could not, flushed by triumph as he was, for-bear adding: "I think little of my own playing."

This veiled reproach was more than Filippo could endure. "Come over yonder where the grass is soft," he muttered through his teeth, and we will see whether you are as good at defending yourself as you are at the pretty amusement of *pome.*"

"You seem rather tired; I noticed you sitting down twice or thrice at the end of our game. Let's put other contests off till other days."

"Coward!" burst out Filippo.

That settled it. They walked slowly and apart to where

the grass was fresh and untrodden underneath some trees. Filippo had brought over his mantle. "You had better bring your coat," he suggested coldly. "Someone might steal it."

The other nodded and went back for it, while Filippo leaned against a tree trunk. When they were together again, the latter slipped out of his tunic, standing only in his shirt and *oricello* hose. The other boy followed suit with his brown and scarlet doublet.

The wrestling match began. Filippo, his pride stung to the quick, seemed not at a disadvantage now. True, very unusual for him, his breath almost at once came in short gasps, he that could ordinarily run a mile without panting. But when his opponent succeeded in tripping him, he was on top before they struck the ground.

The two rolled over and over, each trying to get a grip that would hold the other helpless. Now one was on his back, now the other; now the one, now the other was risen to his knees.

With a mighty effort the stranger lurched to his feet, dragging Filippo with him. They grappled there for a moment, then he managed to fling Filippo again to earth, himself on top. He had his knee on the panting chest.

"Are you beaten?"

"Never!"

Nevertheless, Filippo lay passive beneath the knee. "Now for a grip that will make him know he's done for," thought the other. His two hands imprisoned Filippo's two arms, and he made an effort to bend the latter upwards and across, so that he might at last grasp the throat and make his adversary cry, "Enough!"

It was Filippo's chance. A violent wrench freed one arm;

instantly it was encircling the other's neck; and with a heave of his body he had reversed their positions. The struggle grew truly fierce as he felt himself so near total exhaustion. To be beaten for a second time by this easy-spoken stranger with the familiar face! Never!

They had staggered to their feet again, and by a dexterous move Filippo threw his foe. Down he came on top of him, and almost to his own surprise found himself uppermost. More than that, he had at last got him in a wrestling grip he knew as almost unbreakable. He twisted tight, and gasped as his adversary had done:

"Are you beaten?"

And the same word he himself had given came in answer: "Never!"

Filippo shut his eyes, feeling very weak. Could he keep his hold? In a sort of trance he was aware that the other still struggled, was breaking loose. He gripped very hard at something, and whispered brokenly: "Do… you… give… in?"

From far away a very gentle and tender voice seemed to say:

"Yes, dearest Filippo, my friend, to you."

V

More Than Gold

*S*er Guido de' Nerli, Filippo's father, when his wife had died in Filippo's early childhood, had decided to live a mile or two above Florence in the Fiesolan hills. His brother, Domenico de' Nerli, could never understand his not preferring to be one of *his* big household, which, after the more usual Florentine manner, was made up of several generations of the family. But Ser Guido delighted in the brisk morning and evening rides to and from Florence, in his beautiful views, and in the gardens surrounding his *casa*, where he grew grapes, olives, and other fruits for his own use. "Filippo can very well study with your children, and ride back and forth as I do," he told Domenico; and so it had long been done.

On the following morning, which was Saturday, two boys were lying in the sun on a flower-covered terraced slope, where grape-vines swung between olive trees. On coming out here, the fair-haired lad had spread a robe for the other, which he insisted upon his using.

"Nonsense," said the dark-haired boy, looking affectionately at the other; "you have treated me since yesterday as if I were an invalid or a delicate maiden."

"I cannot help it," returned the other, throwing himself

down beside his companion. "To think of finding you again, as I did, my dearest Filippo!"

"When did you first recognize me, my Giovanni?"

"I have told you already; it was almost at the end of our match that it flashed upon me that you were Filippino, the first friend of my boyhood, and the dearest. I was sure of it when you were lying there all but unconscious, gripping your own limbs in the thought they were mine, with that heart of yours that never says die, and still muttering, 'Do you give in?' Oh, I was happy then, but frightened, too, for I did not know what you had been through to make you take our bout so hard."

"My sweet friend! I understand now all friendship means; to be able to tell you all—you at least won't think now that I am but an idle boaster, as my ridiculous conduct seemed to make me out."

"I did not find it ridiculous," said Giovanni loyally. "I would have loved you for a friend had you not been *you*."

"'A man without a friend is like a body without a soul,'" quoted Filippo. "You were somehow familiar to me from the first. Strange I did not place you."

"Less strange than on my part, for you were weary. How delightful of your father to say you need not go down to your uncle's today, and to invite me to stay over the weekend."

"Oh, father is very hospitable; he'd be charmed to have you stay a month, which I hope you will with all my heart. As for sending me down to Florence, he never does that; he gives me my own way completely. He's fairly wrapped up, first in his law, and second, in our little estate here. He likes to get out and prune a tree or plant a flower-bed himself."

"Yes, I remember him like that. It seems that we must become acquainted all over again."

"Not strange! when we were only eight when we parted. Ah, *amico*, have you kept the ring I gave you then?"

"Here it is around my neck—see? It is too small for my finger, you can believe!"

"And here is mine. Giovanni, you have the same sweet temper you had always. You are not at all like that Neri Picciolin whom Cecco Angiolieri put in verse:

> "When Neri Picciolin came back from France
> He was so full of florins and pride
> That he looked upon men but as poor little mice,
> And each he did mock and deride.
> "He frequently cried, 'Now may evil befall
> All my neighbors, for seen face to face
> With me, they appear but so mean and so small
> That their friendship will bring me disgrace.'"

"My father and I only stayed a month in France," laughed Giovanni with Filippo, "and then we went on to other countries, so the rhyme doesn't hold. Besides, I recall Messer Neri was well punished for his conceit, 'and that ere eight months had gone by, he'd have thanked for a crust flung him down,' as the poem says… Bah, France and England seem countries half-civilized in comparison with our Florence."

"But since your father was doing so brilliantly abroad, why did he return to Florence?"

"'Tis because I didn't take to being a merchant like himself. I have set my heart on being an artist, and he has put me now to study with our great Andrea del Verrocchio."

"San Niccolo! you don't tell me! How do you like it?"

"It is like heaven," rejoined Giovanni fervently. "Messer Andrea is wonderful. And his *bottega* is full of gifted artists."

"I haven't done so very much with art myself," said Filippo. "I seem to take more to literature. I sometimes think that if I were not so lazy I could write something really worth while. Messer my teacher thinks so, and also, my uncle. That reminds me, *amico mio*, that I must write out a poem I have composed on Florentine liberty."

"I will get your writing-case for you. No, do let me. You mustn't tire yourself today."

Giovanni pushed Filippo back when he would have followed, and ran to the house. Filippo smiled after him, and taking up the guitar lying at his side, touched the strings and began to sing. Giovanni joined in the song in the distance. He returned in no time with several articles in his arms. One was a book of poems in manuscript, one a lute, and one the writing-case.

"Ah, but you must listen to my verses, friend, and not divert yourself reading real poetry," chided Filippo with a merry glance. "I want your suggestions."

"Is your poem in Latin, Greek, or our present-day language? I have very little Greek at my command, I must tell you."

"'Tis Latin," returned Filippo, busily writing. "There, there, my dear friend, I did not mean it seriously about not reading to yourself. Do so; for I have to write down eighty lines before I can read them."

"If you have to do that much, I will compose a sonnet or two on our lovely view of Florence from this height. You can imagine how beautiful she is to me when I have only been seeing her for six days after being away for six years."

Filippo nodded, too busy to look up from his work, while Giovanni, plucking the wild flowers at his side, gazed delightedly down at the City of Flowers, "the loveliest of cities," with its rising towers, its enclosing walls, and winding Arno River, the fertile valley, and the encircling hills and distant mountains.

In this way the morning passed until the hour for *comestio*, when the friends walked arm in arm to the house, laughing, and quoting and composing clever epigrams in Greek and Latin. Country life was very simple and healthful, and they helped Monna Nannina and her old mother get the meal. They brought olive oil from the enormous red jar in the storeroom, big enough for a man to hide in, and a supply of fruit preserves in wine.

"What do you say to eating in the arbor, Master Filippo?" queried Nannina.

"It is very pretty, Giovanni," said the host turning to his friend. So the places for the two boys were laid a few feet from the house, on a table beneath vines clothed in the tender green of spring, and fruit and nut trees in flower-bud. There were vegetable soup, bowls of cooked chestnuts with goat's milk, a salad of greens, maccaroni with olive oil and cheese, and fresh and preserved fruits, as delicious a meal as one could wish for.

After it, Giovanni and Filippo amused themselves by making up songs to the sweet music of a lyre, and singing popular *canzoni* in duet while one played on the lute and the other on the guitar. Then they discussed their studies and their tutors, displaying a perfection of speech—and half their talk was in the classical tongues—and a knowledge of literature and the arts that would put to shame our university graduates of today. They quoted and spoke of the "divine" Dante, of Francesco Petrarca or Petrarch, and of Boccaccio—the three greatest names in Italian literature and a Florentine each of them—and they brought in as freely Virgil and Cicero and Plato and other of the immortal writers of ancient Rome and Greece.

Ser Guido, Filippo's kindly and agreeable father, returned in time for *prandium*, and after making that meal entertaining for the boys with his conversation about happenings in the city and his questions about themselves, left them to play a game of chess while he buried himself, not in a book of law, but in a manuscript on how best to grow fruits.

Filippo and Giovanni retired early. As they embraced each other good-night, Filippo promised: "I have an adventure for tomorrow, my Giovanni, that will make you dance with joy!"

In the morning Filippo called for his friend at dawn, and found him sitting on the side of his curtained bed, swinging his heels and already dressed. "Come," said Filippo, "we must pack lunches, for we are off for an adventurous exploring trip today."

"How do you feel, my *buono amico?*" queried Giovanni.

"Never felt better in my life."

"Are you sure?"

"Sure."

"Bravo!" exclaimed Giovanni, and with one more press to each other's hands, the boys raced into the kitchen. Preparations were soon made, and they were off just as the church bells began to ring in the day, which was Palm Sunday.

The scene was exquisite. The flowery hills were still half cloaked in mist, and out of it rose the roofs of the many scattered villas of wealthy Florentines like those of fairy castles, touched with the gold of the rising sun. Even as the boys looked, here this spot and there that came into view as if a veil were withdrawn by unseen hands, showing terraced vineyards and olive orchards, and the houses amongst them. They could look down on the monastery of San Domenico, and on down to Florence just emerging into clear sight, and off to surrounding hills whose steep slopes and ridges were set with walled villages and rising church towers. And further off were the mountains; and above their own heads on the rocky height, the ancient Etruscan town of Fiesole.

They were ascending at a swinging gait the very steep road to this town, which, still filled with ruins of Etruscan and of Roman times, was one of the most ancient towns in all Italy. They had passed the cypresses around the Villa Medici, one of the palaces of the "uncrowned king" who ruled Florence, when they saw coming down upon them a white-robed procession.

"Excellent!" exclaimed Filippo. "See, my friend, the Palm Sunday celebration we have chanced upon."

The two stood off to the side of the road with bared heads to see it pass. It was not a church procession, but one gotten up by pious country-folk. First was borne an image of Christ wreathed in olive branches, flanked by men carrying tall tapers, which they were having difficulty in keeping alight as they came down the steep slope. This was followed by a child leading a donkey, also garlanded with olive, in remembrance that Jesus had ridden upon this humble animal. Then followed men, women, and children, all dressed in white and wearing olive twigs twined around their brows, and holding larger branches of the tree of peace in their hands. As they came near they burst into song, and went through motions as if strewing the branches on the ground before the Saviour's feet. At the end, came again sacred banners, with pictures of Jesus, the Holy Mother, and St. Mary Magdalen.

When Filippo and Giovanni at last came into the central *piazza* of Fiesole, they found a fair in progress. Red-cheeked peasant women were busy making thin Lenten wafers called *brigidini* over brasiers. Others were selling nuts and sweets, and there was much laughing and joking among the early corners, and lovemaking between the *contadini* youths and maidens. But Filippo and Giovanni glanced without particular interest at the gay stalls, most of them still being put up. They followed the people who were entering the open doors of the four-hundred-and-fifty year old cathedral.

When Mass was over, "Now," said Filippo excitedly, "our day begins! I will show you, my Giovanni, a secret not a soul on earth knows but myself."

"Ah, Filippino, I can guess it has to do with the ruins! Is it an unknown vault full of ancient *denarii?*"

"You are too ambitious, *amico*. But see, here *are* some *denarii* I found here last year. I brought them on purpose to show you." Filippo held out five ancient Roman coins.

"*Santa Maria!*" ejaculated Giovanni as he looked at them, "these were coined before Our Lord Jesus Christ was born! And silver, too, though they look as black as night!"

"They are yours, Giovannino."

"Nay, we will divide them."

"How divide five?"—laughing.

"When we return I will cut the fifth in two, and it shall stand for our happiness, which is only complete when we are together."

"They should be of purest gold for that!"

"'Twould not suffice: friendship is more than all the gold our Florence has coined, though that is known to the ends of the earth."

They walked on in a few moments' silence beside the giant Etruscan walls, whose one-and-two-third mile circuit, in 1478, was still withstanding in many places the weight of centuries. The very old town of Fiesole had been a chief city of Etruria (ancient Tuscany) long before Rome began to make herself the mistress of the world; in Roman days it had been for a period a place of wealth and importance, with handsome buildings, statues and temples, public baths and theater, citadel and statehouse. Some of the Roman ruins were still extant, though the last traces of many of them had disappeared when their stone was used for modern buildings here and in Florence. In this way, Christian churches had been made out of Pagan temples, and Florentine palaces out of Roman houses.

"Faesulae was already old when Florentia began," remarked Filippo, using the classic names for the cities. "When one shuts one's eyes to present things, one can imagine yonder columns the front of a temple, a triumphal army passing under that arch there, and this gateway thronging with citizens in togas."

"Can't one, though! And I say, these walls are a marvel. Just look at the size of the blocks! They look as if they had been hewn by giants."

"Aye, this wall must be close to fifteen *braccii* high (nearly thirty feet). What say you, my artist?"

"That to the best of my judgment you are right, but that we cannot very well measure the walls up and down with a stick!"

"Oh, can't we! That is the very thing I am going to have us do a bit further on—with a rope if not with a stick!"

"It sounds like an adventure after mine own heart!"

"Let's begin by pacing out some of these giant blocks of stone. They make one feel as if the Etruscans had been a race of Cyclops to be able to drag them out of their beds in the hill and pile up twelve and fourteen of them atop each other."

"Do you know how long this one is?" asked Giovanni, who had been letting his friend finish his declamation while he acted on his suggestion. "It's more than six *braccii* in length, and one-and-a-half in height!"

"Jupiter! I wish we could have seen the builders move it into place. But here we are, my Giovannino. This is the one place I've been able to find where one can scale the walls."

"Faith! it looks impossible!" cried Giovanni with delight.

Filippo had already set his foot upon a tiny projection, his fingers in another, and in one step was up two and a half feet. "We are enemy spies scaling the wall at dead of night," he whispered, leaping down and flinging an arm about Giovanni. "Do you think you can follow, my Gian? I admit it's a very risky feat."

Giovanni nodded emphatically, and inquired: "Where is the rope to descend the other side—into the midst of the sleeping garrison?"

"Here, about my waist," murmured Filippo, raising his

coat and showing a rope coiled around his waist. "'Tis very light but strong."

"So you really have a rope, my excellent Filippo. I thought you had grown fatter!" laughed Giovanni.

"Hush!" admonished the other, "or we shall be heard."

Filippo again made the first step, then turned back with the serious: "Are you sure you feel certain of yourself, my dear comrade? If you don't, I don't want to drag you up here."

Giovanni did not waste words. With his knee already against the towering wall, he pressed his friend's hand, and sang: "Move up another course, I beg you! I'm behind."

Up, up the boys moved, Filippo feeling out each foothold and fingerhold, Giovanni pressing on just a lap behind. Up, up they continued, like strangely gigantic bugs able to scale the perpendicular, and the wall was now only twenty feet above them and ten below—enough and more for a slip to the rocky ground to be one's last.

The sun beat hotly upon the stones. The lads were more like worms as they rose higher, clinging still more closely to the surface as they felt themselves grow a little dizzy at thought of their danger. Sometimes they could not but catch their breaths as they found it necessary to wriggle up an unusually high step. Yet Filippo must know this "stairway," Giovanni was aware; he followed, confident of his friend.

Not one word had been spoken since the ascent began. Throats were too dry and tense to speak unless they must. All energy went into straining fingers and toes and knees.

They were within ten feet of the top. Then, by one more lift of the body from block to block, eight. Filippo paused for a longer moment than usual, causing Giovanni to pause also.

It was impossible, balancing as Filippo was on an infinitesimal ledge of rock, to turn his head. "Are you safe?" he asked, his voice coming harshly from his dry mouth.

"Yes."

"It's the hardest of all here. You must wait. I'll get up and throw you a rope."

"I'll come with you," refused Giovanni.

"No. It isn't safe, I tell you. Wait."

"Please, for my sake. I can't do it myself if I think you're in danger."

Giovanni had a great longing to face the danger abreast with his dear comrade, but Filippo blocked the only route up. "If you feel that way, *amico,*" said Giovanni, "I'll wait."

He felt his own limbs tremble as he watched Filippo. He saw first one hand go up, and up, stretched to its full extent. The fingers were scarcely resting on a ledge. Could they ever hold?

Then the other hand—up, up, to rest beside the first.

It took all Giovanni's power of will to keep from screaming out. Only the realization that to do so would probably send his beloved friend toppling to earth, kept the cry in check. "Holy Mother, Mother of Christ, protect him now," he prayed with all his soul.

Filippo had raised himself by the muscles of his arms so that his chin rested on the jutting bit of rock. His feet and body hung absolutely in the air.

Then, the weight of his body hanging by his chin, he again stretched one arm and then the other up. Clinging to the new fingerhold, he raised himself once more by his muscles, slowly, painfully, it seemed to Giovanni, yet higher, higher, until at last—"Mary be praised!" cried Giovanni—one foot, yes, both feet, were safely on the new hold.

Stopping for a few breaths, Filippo scaled the last few feet of wall with comparative ease, even to pulling himself atop the mighty structure. He backed out of sight, then his head re-appeared, and the knotted rope came slowly down towards Giovanni. Filippo called cheerily: "Rope's perfectly secure; I've got it round a rock and my coat at the bend so it won't wear through."

With this assurance, Giovanni swung up hand over hand, and was quickly beside his friend. "I can't figure how more than one of us can get down here without leaving the rope and my coat," Filippo greeted him. "I'm afraid we must be olden soldiers for a while, manning the walls. If we walk along here a way we'll come to an easy route down." He began to wind the rope about his waist again.

"Wait," said Giovanni. "We'll tie a stone to that and drop it. You've forgotten that we were going to measure the wall."

When this was done, and rope and lunches once more made secure, the boys clambered forward along the uneven roof of the wall, taking turns in reciting stanzas from the popular epic which told of the knightly days of Charlemagne, and especially of his three heroes, Rinaldo with his famed horse Bayard, and Orlando and Oliviero who had been friends even to death. This was the Italian version of the French "Song of Roland," and ended up, if one ever got as far as the end, with the tragic battle of Roncesvalles, and the Emperor avenging his slain peers.

"Here we are," said Filippo, as they came to the end of their strip of wall. It tapered off quite gently, and they bounded down from jutting rock to rock as easily as mountain goats. "Now," he added, throwing his arm about Giovanni's neck and turning him towards a barren pile of huge stones lying against the rocky slope, "here is our real adventure!"

"Ah!"

"Here I found the *denarii*. Quickly, come!" He looked around. No one was in sight in this outskirt of the little town. Everyone, doubtless, was praying in church or making merry at the fair. Taking off his coat—he had been wise enough to wear a rough jerkin beneath it today—he crawled on hands and knees amongst the boulders. Giovanni imitated him in all particulars.

They found themselves behind a big stone, in a sort of hollow, a cold and dismal spot. Their way was blocked on three sides, but Filippo, using his knife, chipped at the rocks at his feet.

"Gloria!" cried Giovanni beneath his breath; for, as Filippo lifted a larger rock, he looked down into a black hole.

"This is my excavation," explained Filippo quite unnecessarily, for Giovanni's glowing eyes showed he knew it as well as his friend.

"How deep can you go?"

"It's a passage. I've never dared go to the end. That's for us to do today."

"Bravo!"

"We'll eat our meal first." The boys went back into the sunlight and made a good repast from their bread, cheese, and fruit. Then taking their wraps with them, they laid them beside the hole.

"You can jump down," said Filippo. "I dug this part out myself. It's soft earth. The masonry begins further on."

Giovanni had not waited for him to finish. Filippo landed beside him, and continued: "We'll light candles." He drew a tinder-box from his *scarsella*, struck a spark, and held the wick of a small taper to it. Handing this to Giovanni, he lighted a second from it.

"Well! you are well prepared!" exclaimed Giovanni.

"Better than you think—for I have a spade and a pick stored further on in here."

Giovanni, peering into the flickering shadows, saw that a round passageway opened off to one side. "It looks to me like nothing so much as an ancient sewer."

Filippo shook his head. "I doubt it."

"I'll lead," proposed Giovanni; but when he saw Filippo's look of disappointment, he quickly added: "No, you should lead, since it is your find."

Filippo shot him a glance of appreciation, and one after the other they made their way into the passageway, along which they had to proceed bent nearly double. What a feeling! One seemed to be walking miles underground. A chill current of air followed them, "And the smell," whispered Giovanni, "seems to be centuries old."

At a bend, they came upon Filippo's spade and pick. Each silently shouldered one of the implements. The corridor had risen in height and flattened out beneath their feet. "Perhaps this was made by the early Christians when they were persecuted, and leads to one of their secret meeting places."

"We'll find out—if our breath lasts. Don't you find your breathing hard, my Giovanni?"

"That I do. And see how dimly our tapers burn."

They walked on, abreast now, in the heavy echoing silence, that seemed to hem them in and weigh them down like something living.

"This is as far as I've gone," announced Filippo suddenly, as, making a turn, they found their way blocked.

"It doesn't look as if we could get through," returned Giovanni disappointedly.

"I think we can. Hold your candle up."

Both boys raised their candles, moving them about. At one place the flames leaped up brightly. "There is air coming through here! Hold the lights and I'll take a try with the pick."

After some minutes hard labor, Filippo admitted: "Can't seem to make any progress. See what you can do, my friend."

Giovanni carefully searched the obstructing mass with his light. Then pushing in his pick as a pry, he gave a tug. "It is moving!" the friends exclaimed together as the center stone budged.

"Take care it doesn't come down on us!" cautioned Filippo.

"I'm keeping that in mind."

Giovanni continued working, slowly and carefully, from the top down. He tested the rocks from time to time to see how secure they were. He deliberately piled up those he had succeeded in extracting. Although he was working longer than Filippo had, because with less violent effort, he seemed to be making hardly more headway.

"My turn," said Filippo, and taking his place, gave a strong blow with his pick.

"Don't! Don't do that!" ejaculated Giovanni, seizing his arm. "You'll bring the whole roof down on us!"

As if in answer to his warning there was the crash of falling stones. The friends, plunged into darkness, toppled back.

Nothing further was heard. Succeeding in striking new lights, they looked around.

"Here! Here!" screamed Filippo, beside himself with joy. "See! See!"

Giovanni already saw, and met Filippo's eager hug. "It is the find of a lifetime!"

They were gazing, flushed cheek by flushed cheek, through a small hole into a stone vault.

"Who knows what treasures of antiquity are there!"

"We must get in!" cried Filippo, and began almost wildly to enlarge the aperture.

"Careful! Careful!" urged Giovanni, as the whole tunnel seemed to tremble. *"Perdio!!!"*—this last as a chip of stone hit his neck. "Have patience, Filippo! You're too headstrong; we've got all afternoon for this."

Fillipo paid no attention except to shout: "Back, step back, Gian! I must have room for my pick."

Giovanni did so, and stood watching. The hole grew bigger and bigger.

"I'll get this rock, and there'll be space enough."

"Better make sure the sides are safe, first."

"They're all right," muttered Filippo through clenched teeth as he devoted all his effort to his pick. "Hold those lights higher, will you, Gian!"

After a moment of concentrated effort; "It's coming!" he exulted.

"Run! Run!" screamed Giovanni.

Filippo whirled round at the warning, but tripped over the spade and fell flat on his face.

With a wild inarticulate cry, Giovanni sprang forward to protect him, hands upraised. At the same instant, the side walls as well as the divided front one collapsed. Human shrieks were lost in the roar.

For moments the clang and reverberations of the crash filled the ears like an ocean. Then, from under the mass of stones and earth, Filippo's weak and agonized voice sobbed to the body across his: "Giovannino! Giovannino! You aren't dead? Oh, you've given your life for mine! O God, take me too."

VI

Behold the Miracle!

Giovanni, buried in the ruins with Filippo, had only been stunned and not killed. The slabs of rock had mercifully met together, forming a V-shaped space of safety beneath. But when he stirred on Filippo's back, he came to himself with groans, for in protecting Filippo his left hand had been broken at the wrist.

Then followed a period of awful torture for the boys. With death hanging over them, as it were, by a hair, they dared not move a finger lest they be crushed. Filippo tried to call out for help, but with his face held down by the rocks to the ground, he knew his feeble cries could hardly be heard a *braccio* away. He felt Giovanni's body throb and quiver, and hardly knew whether his friend was conscious or not except for an occasional moan of great pain Giovanni could not keep back. Giovanni, on top, in the narrower part of the V, was wedged in so tightly that he could not even lift his broken wrist to his chest or touch it with his other hand. He too tried to call once or twice, but the effort was beyond his power.

Thus, in darkness, torment, and despair, passed what seemed hours. Giovanni must have slept or fainted for a time. Great as was his pain, perhaps it was not he but Filippo who suffered the more, for Filippo had the anguish of feeling he was responsible for his friend's fate. He tried to calm himself enough to think over what chances of rescue they had, and they seemed to him non-existent. He tried to say something to Giovanni, but he could no longer speak. He thought he was suffocating, or may be it was dying.

All at once the sound of voices broke confusedly on his ear. As in a dream he listened to them. They were cheerful peasant voices, a man's and a woman's, and seemed greatly excited:

"Will you just look at our cellar, good-wife! I come down to bring up the wine, and here's how it is!"

"Saints protect us! If there was an earth-quake we didn't feel it at the fair."

With a violent effort Filippo shook off the spell and gave a groan for help. "Rescue! We're buried under!"

* * * * * * * * * *

Both lads were thinking of this experience as they rode slowly down to Florence on Tuesday morning. Giovanni on Sunday evening had passed through the hard ordeal of having his wrist set and splintered, and at Ser Guido's insistence, had spent Monday also with Filippo.

Filippo could hardly keep the tears back from his eyes whenever he looked at the arm in its cast and sling. "I don't see how you can be so sweet-tempered, Giovannino!" he exclaimed. "You did so much for me, and I don't even know how to tell you how grateful and how sorry I am. How can you forgive me?"

"*Forgive* you, my beloved Filippo when this has only made our friendship all the dearer."

"I, through the selfish risks I took, nearly killed us both, and you offered your life for mine."

Giovanni pulled his horse still closer to Filippo, and said softly: "Don't speak so, *amico;* what does it matter who first has the chance to serve the other?" Then, smiling, he changed the subject: "That was the most amusing thing I ever heard of, about our antique vault! Think of it being already known, and in use as an ordinary wine-cellar! *Perdio*, all the noble statues and other treasures we expected to find, were nothing but Tuscan wine barrels!"

"Well, anyway," remarked Filippo, joining in the laugh, "the passage and vault were at least genuine ancient ruins. Doubtless there *were* valuable discoveries there at one time or another."

They were entering Florence by the Porta San Gallo (San Gallo Gate), when Filippo bent far from the saddle to pick up a couple of rocks from the road. A cat was running along the street some distance ahead. "Watch," he said; "I'll make that creature jump."

Just as the rock was about to fly from his hand, Giovanni threw his horse across the way and seized the arm. The missile dropped harmlessly.

"What on earth!" exclaimed Filippo in surprise. "You'll hurt your wrist, *amico!*"

"I did do so already," returned Giovanni, his lips twisted by pain. "But that is far better than having a poor thing suffer that is much weaker than myself."

"But—but—it's only a cat."

"Don't you think a cat can feel as much pain or perhaps more than we can? I know what pain is," he added with a rueful smile.

Filippo's face suddenly flushed crimson as he looked at

Giovanni's arm, for he realized the truth of his words. "I was a coward," he said. "It was a shameful act—for I too know what pain and suffering are… Still," he continued, the usual careless attitude towards animals struggling with these new feelings, "still, animals are so far beneath us…"

"Are they?" asked Giovanni pointedly. "Don't you think our great Petrarca's cat, whom he loved so well, was a better friend to him than many faithless human ones? Don't you think Saint Roch's little dog, who brought him food every day when he was stricken by the plague, did more than many a Christian? Lorenzo the Magnificent has a horse that is so devoted to him it will eat only from his own hand."

Giovanni paused, and then went on: "It seems to me that we are only higher than animals when we are not only wiser than they are, but *better*. And we are not better unless we are merciful to them. All animals are so weak and helpless compared with us. As you just said, to hurt one is the act of a coward…"

Filippo's cheeks reddened again at the word, but he was silent. "To cause pain to anything weaker than oneself is cowardly," emphasized Giovanni. "But don't think, dearest Filippo, that I am chiding you. I have done what you were about to do, and worse, too, though I have always had a sort of pity for animals. But since I have come back from abroad, I have talked with a wonderful young artist who is a friend and former pupil of my master, Andrea del Verrocchio. You know him, for already everyone in Florence is speaking about his painting; his name is Leonardo da Vinci."

"I have seen him on the streets," nodded Filippo. "He *is* wonderful. In beauty and grace he looks like a Greek god."

"And he's so strong that he can bend an iron horseshoe like a reed. He can tame the wildest horse and make it obey him like a dog. He can sing and compose to the lyre like an angel. Everybody, from the highest to the lowest, loves him. There seems nothing he cannot do. He is master of every subject; and Messer Andrea says that his name will shine in art as no name has ever shone before. Besides painting and sculpturing, he's marvellous in architecture and engineering and philosophy and music and mathematics and fencing and in everything else; I think there never was such a man."

"What does he say about animals?"

"Monday of last week, when I first came to Messer Andrea's *bottega*, Leonardo was there, and when I was going home invited me to walk with him to the *Serraglio*. As we were looking at the lions, I remarked that I really hated to see them in captivity, when they had been used to roaming as they willed in their native jungles. Then he told me that he buys the wild birds that are sold in the market-places, and sets them free. Nearly every day he has taken me to the Mercato Vecchio or the Mercato Nuovo where we have bought several cages full, and taken them up in the hills and opened the doors. It makes one very happy to see the poor wild creatures stare around, unable to believe their happy fate, and at last stretch their wings and soar away."

"By my faith, it's true they must be miserable in the cages when they were born free."

"Leonardo has also spoken to me much about animals. He feeds them in bitter winter, when he says they come to the door just like starving human beggars asking for alms. He would not hurt the tiniest living creature. He read me

WE HAVE TAKEN SEVERAL CAGES FULL UP IN
THE HILLS AND OPENED THE DOORS.

something he wrote on the cruelty of Man, 'an animal always warring against his own species, persecuting, harassing, and devastating all things that are on the earth or beneath it or in the water.'—It's true, isn't it? And it's hardly believable, but he does not even eat meat, because he does not wish animals killed for him. I don't go that far myself, because death isn't horrible to think of, as are suffering and torture. Perhaps though, some day I'll be like Leonardo in that also."

They had drawn up beside the wall as they spoke, and now they rode over to the hostel and dismounted. Leaving their horses with the inn-keeper, they went forward on foot down the wide street called Via Larga. They walked almost in silence as far as San Marco, where Filippo turned to Giovanni with: "I wouldn't have stood the word 'coward' from anyone else on earth, but I'm glad you used it."

Filippo arrived at his uncle's house well supplied with manuscripts for his tutor. First there was the eighty-line Latin poem, then an essay, also in Latin, entitled "The Ideal Government", and last a long translation from Homer, Greek into Latin. A servant unbolted the stout oaken door, and Filippo passed through several finely decorated rooms opening into each other, to the library. Messer Cosimo had not come in yet, but four cousins swooped upon the new arrival.

"Filippo!" "Lippo!" "Lippo you rascal!" "Filippino!" The three boys, the eldest a trifle younger than he, and the girl circled around him dancing. "Ah, we have been hearing tales about you drowning yourself in the Arno and finding old friends and I don't know what all," said the girl cousin, Margherita. "I don't believe you love us anymore."

"You lucky wretch," grinned Mariano, the oldest boy, "you've missed doing any lessons for half a week."

"But see, he has scrolls with him," spoke up little Luca.

"Ah," said Michele, "have you committed any further 'heresies,' Filippo? That is, have you written your manuscripts there in the modern language, which our Master scorns so, or spoken slightingly of his favorite classics?"

"Ha, ha!" chuckled Mariano. "There never was anyone like our Filippo for badgering our worthy Master! Ha, ha! Messer Cosimo never sees through it, either."

Filippo shook his head. "I've been thinking on it these last days, and I'm not going to tease our Master again. I'm going to study hard and be a credit to him—which I advise you to do too, Cousin Mariano." He added this last rather pointedly, for Mariano was not a very brilliant scholar.

Neither Mariano nor Michele looked particularly pleased. Studies were dull things, and clever and gifted Filippo had formerly livened them up. But Margherita smiled sweetly at him and offered him her hand: "I just know you can do wonders, Filippino, if you only want to."

"I'm glad," said little Luca, putting his arms about his tall and handsome cousin. "I think it was mean the way you all played jokes on Messer Cosimo. He is very learned and wise, and he's old, too, and so gentle and good. I love him."

"I do, too, "said Filippo with feeling, giving his "baby" cousin a kiss just as Messer Cosimo himself entered the room.

And that morning, for the first time, Filippo realized how much he did love the fine old scholar who was their teacher. He was so tender as he asked Filippo about his weekend adventures, and, when he examined the manuscripts, praised them so warmly. Filippo really felt rather shamed by the latter, and at last burst out with: "I wish you wouldn't praise them so much, my master; I know how little time I put into them and how much better I could have done if I'd only tried."

To Filippo's surprise, Messer Cosimo seemed overcome by emotion. He wiped his eyes, and was only able to say brokenly: "My boy, my boy, you will be famous one day."

"If I ever am, Messere, it will be owing to you.,,

Following the Greek ideal of education, Messer Cosimo put very little restraint on his pupils. After an hour or so of studying in the library, filled with its treasure of books in manuscript and two or three printed copies, though printing-presses were but a few years old in Florence, he took the children into the garden. After a short recess of practicing swordsman-ship and leaping and other exercises, he called them to the stone bench where he was sitting, and discussed with them what they had studied that day. Filippo sat at the master's feet, Margherita had brought a cushion for herself, and one for Messer Cosimo's bench, and the three brothers sat together on another bench, supported by carved figures of lions. It was very pleasant learning in the beautiful old garden, with its flagged walks and rose-vines and orange and cypress trees.

After eating *comestio* indoors, the teacher retired for a rest, giving his pupils each a task: Luca to memorize some verses from Virgil, Michele to study in the second book of Teodoro Gaza's Greek grammar, and Margherita, Mariano, and Filippo each to put some passages from Dante's *Commedia* into Greek. They all trouped out into the garden again, where lying on the grass among the flower-beds, they set to work.

Filippo was very quickly through. Putting away his pen and books, he brought out a lute and wandering to a further corner of the garden, played softly to himself. This sight was extremely galling to Mariano and Michele, for they found their own, and easier, passages most difficult.

"Ah ha," suggested Mariano to his brother, "don't I remember Filippo vowing he'd never have to study during Holy Week, that he'd have the whole Sunday-to-Sunday for vacation? Yet here he's been all day, studying just like the rest of us!"

"He said last week that if Messer—our teacher—didn't give him this week off, there'd be a miracle that would make him. He said Heaven was on his side because he wanted to spend the week in church-going and prayer, but I think myself he wanted the time for playing ball."

"Let's go to him and ask why his miracle hasn't come off, whether Heaven's angry at him!"

Filippo had, in fact, forgotten all about the miracle joke for which he had bought the red powder, when the two boys descended on him with an avalanche of sarcastic questions. "The miracle's all off," he answered carelessly. "I went to church so often over the weekend that Heaven has forgiven Messer Cosimo for not giving me a vacation."

"It's off because Messer Cosimo coddled you so this morning and praised your work as if it had been written by the great Angelo Poliziano himself. Some people are easily flattered."

Filippo flushed angrily. "It isn't that, Mariano. I am not making my miracle—I see you know it was I and not Heaven—because I agree with little Luca now that it is mean to torment our Master. If you and Michele were studying your lessons instead of nagging me, you would be doing better."

"It's easy for you to talk!" snapped Michele, "a boy who doesn't keep his word."

"Yes, you *promised* the miracle," insisted Mariano.

Filippo went red and white with rage. "I should like to knock your two heads together," he muttered. "Well—I'll give you the miracle. Go and tell Margherita there'll be one."

Filippo had arranged the whole apparatus for his jest the preceding week. When they went into the library again with Messer Cosimo, he had nothing to do but fill the hollow figure of a dove he had made, with the red fire powder, light it, and send it flying on the thin wire which was invisible to the teacher's old eyes. He had got the idea partly from the celebration held in the cathedral each year on Holy Saturday. Well, it would be very pretty and effective, the room suddenly blazing up in red glory, the shining white dove hovering in the red haze like a messenger from on high.

They returned to the room. Messer Cosimo stood before his *leggio* or reading-desk, an open book before him, clad in his flowing black gown and scull-cap. His pupils sat about the room, writing materials on their knees. Filippo knew the Master was far too absorbed in the learning he was expounding, to see him. He slyly drew out the dove from under his seat, and screening it with his body, filled it with the powder, which was still in its package in his leather *scarsella;* the excellently made purse did not show it had been wet. Then, on pretence of wanting a drink of water, he left the room and came back with a lighted coal in an eggshell.

He attached the dove to the wire, and dropped the coal

through the trap in its back. A touch sent the bird skimming along the wire, its white wings quivering. There was a faint sputter, and Filippo thought he already saw the red smoke coming.

"Behold!" he cried. "Behold the miracle!"

"Behold the miracle!" his cousins joined in, Luca, Margherita, Michele, and Mariano.

But the dove simply hovered in the air, no red blaze of glory about it, nothing. The powder *had* been spoiled by its bath.

Shouts turned to laughter. "Behold the miracle, ha ha!" "Behold the miracle that didn't work!" "Vain Filippo! we fear you're no Saint!"

"What, what is it, my children?" queried the old teacher, peering at them in astonishment. "Is this a time to play?"

"The matter is," said Filippo, walking straight up to his desk and speaking so that the room could hear, "is that I deserve to be thrashed. This is one of a hundred or more jokes I have played on you, and which you, in your goodness of heart, have failed to suspect me of."

"My Filippo…" quavered the old man.

Filippo bowed his proud head on the desk and kissed the teacher's hands which lay there. "And, Master—Father, I swear to you it will be the last."

VII

In Danger

Holy Week was proving itself a very happy time to Filippo and Giovanni. On Thursday evening when the two friends met at the door of Verrocchio's studio, Filippo said: "You will spend the night with me, and we will be together all day tomorrow." Thus they again rode together up the Fiesolan hills, amid the soft green grass of spring, the gay wild flowers in their reds and blues and yellows, the white oxen finishing the day's plowing, the grape-vines swinging between the olive trees on the terraced slopes, the happy peasants singing as they trudged homewards, and all the other attractive things of country life.

With morning they were again down in Florence. It was Good Friday, the twentieth of March. The boys were almost moved to tears by the special service in the great cathedral. On the altar was a representation of Christ crucified on Calvary, with the weeping Marys about Him and the two thieves on crosses by His side. The fine organ, marvellously played, filled the dim and lofty interior of the church with sad music. The voices of the famous choir of singers rose and fell in the sacred songs of lament. But after this service, Filippo and Giovanni spent several hours wandering to the other important churches of the city, for in each of them there were different representations for the day, Christ carrying the cross, the Roman guards, His Mother and Saint John the Beloved bidding Him farewell, and so on in great number. They enjoyed it all like a religious play, for some of the scenes were quite lovely as works of art.

In the streets they also saw a church procession. It was carrying the celebrated Silver Cross of the beautiful Silver Altar of the Baptistery (the church of San Giovanni Battista, opposite the cathedral). This cross was supposed to contain a piece of the Holy Cross itself. Little acolytes dressed in white walked beside it, bearing lighted tapers. Then there were clergy in rich gold and crimson and white vestments, priests, and many monks. When all had passed out of sight around the corner they could still be heard chanting.

"That reminds me," suggested Filippo. "Let's go to one of the gates and see a *contadini* procession."

Passing the time telling stories and reciting poetry, they left the center of town and wandered through the partly settled suburbs and out the third circle of strong stone walls. They had chosen the gate well, for they had hardly left it behind when they caught sight of a body of people winding toward them from one of the outlying villages. Already they could hear the weeping and wailing. "They're carrying the dead Christ," said Filippo. "Do you remember how they do?"

The peasant procession came nearer. In its midst was a figure borne on a bier. About it were men dressed as Roman soldiers, carrying round shields and pikes. They represented the Roman guard. Around them, again, were women and other men, as well as many children, carrying armfuls of flowers and sobbing and lamenting as if the figure were really the dead Jesus. It was a picturesque sight.

"Today everything is weeping and sadness," observed Filippo; "tomorrow at noon all will be brightness and joy."

"But what say you, my dear friend, that we for our part have had enough melancholy to-day? Messer Andrea is holding open house this afternoon, and I know his former pupil Leonardo da Vinci will be there, and others who are interesting. Would you care to come?"

"What a question, *amico!* You know I have been dying to meet your fascinating Leonardo and your master, too."

"Well and good!" They strolled the considerable way back to the center of Florence. Andrea Verrocchio's studio, a large affair of several rooms, was today not humming with the work of the master and his assistants and pupils as they executed masterpieces in bronze and marble and paint (for Andrea, like most Florentine artists, was a many-sided genius), but was buzzing instead with voices in merry conversation. It was a gathering made up of artists famous or soon to be famous.

Verrocchio, a man in the prime of life with a remarkable, strong, square-cut face and kindly eyes, greeted the boys. "Sit where you like, my lads; hear all you can, for in that way lies wisdom; and help yourselves to refreshments to the full content of your palates—if your stomachs will let you." With these genial words and the friendly twinkle in his eyes, he made them at home.

In truth it was a wonderful opportunity for two talented boys who loved art and were interested in everything. About the room, with its castings in bronze and half completed marble statues, were a number of Florence's most famous living artists. "Look," whispered Giovanni in wonder, "at that old man with his arm on the younger man's shoulder. That is Luca della Robbia, with his nephew Andrea. Who would have guessed he would come out today?"

Filippo looked at the seventy-nine year old sculptor, who had invented the beautiful new finish of colored glaze for his admirable works in terra-cotta. Giovanni was continuing: "And see, there is Il Ghirlandajo, who can never get enough of painting, and says he wishes he were given a commission to paint the whole circuit of the walls of Florence!" Filippo turned to the dark man who was popularly called by this title, meaning The Garland-Maker, because he had started his distinguished career as an artist, by being a goldsmith making carved wreaths of gold and silver.

"That youth there of eighteen with the gentle face is Lorenzo di Credi, my master's pupil. The slightly older youth he talks to is Filippino Lippi. Those men beyond them are the two Pollaiuoli. And there is the foreign artist we call Il Perugino, from the city he comes from in Umbria. He is very poor," whispered Giovanni still lower; "they say he cannot even afford a bed but has to sleep on a chest. But look at his face; he knows he has genius and will be known some day."

Thus Giovanni pointed out the guests, some already with many years of renown behind them, some just beginning to carve out for themselves the names that would make them world-known. He did not point out Leonardo da Vinci, for he saw Filippo's eyes were already upon him and seemed unable to tear themselves away. That was the power of Leonardo. Every person in the room seemed under the spell of his radiant face and singularly charming manner. Filippo saw him as a young man of twenty-five, dressed in a short rose tunic, with golden hair waving to his shoulders. He thought him more beautiful than the Greek god Apollo.

"I recognize the artist sitting beside Leonardo," said Filippo, biting into a piece of delicious pastry, and motioning with it to the young man with short hair curling about his ears. "It is the acclaimed Sandro Botticelli."

"Ah, yes, he is a close friend of Leonardo's. And look now, what Leonardo is doing to him! Those two are always playing some merry joke."

Filippo saw that as Leonardo talked, he was slyly drawing a sketch on Botticelli's back with red chalk, unknown to the latter. "By the way, my dear Sandro," said Leonardo, putting a last touch to the picture, "you remember we had a wager a month or two ago as to which of us would *not* finish the picture he was engaged on, first. I have hardly done a stroke more on my Two Madonnas, and you, I hear, have quite completed your masterpiece for Lorenzo de' Medici."

"True," nodded Sandro.

"And our wager was," persisted Leonardo, smiling merrily, "tunic to jerkin."

"I admit it," said Sandro.

"Well, my friend, I publicly hold you to the bargain, and demand that you surrender to me the jerkin that is henceforth mine."

"What! take it off in the presence of this excellent company."

"To be sure," smiled Leonardo. "It proves you a man of honor."

"Ho! ho!" laughed Andrea Verrocchio heartily, "that pays you back, Messer Sandro, for some good jokes of your own!"

The company roared. "I give it up grudgingly, mind," affirmed Botticelli, as a number of hands helped him remove his jerkin. Leonardo, standing up, took the garment and leaped lightly on a table. "Good friends," he said, putting on a pretendedly very serious, not to say tragic, air, "it is an extremely melancholy, a most pathetic sight to see one of Florence's leading artists standing amongst us in his undershirt. We are all artists, and some of us are poor, but not one of us is so poor that he must go without a doublet or jerkin. For that reason I ask your compassion for Alessandro Botticelli. See, here is a fine garment belonging to me, Leonardo da Vinci, and attractively adorned by a sketch of mine in red chalk—" He held the jerkin up so that all could see its back except the ex-owner.

"Now," he continued, "I will present this interesting garment as a gift from this company to Andrea del Verrocchio, friend of us all and teacher to many of us, if you, magnificent citizens of the Republic, will each contribute a *denaro* to poor dear Sandro, to buy him a rag or two to cover himself with. Here, Lorenzo my friend, pass around a cap for the purpose."

How the artists did laugh! The very walls and roof seemed to shake with their merriment. All crowded trying to see the picture on the jerkin, including Sandro, but though Leonardo showed it willingly to the others, each time Sandro tried to look he snatched it round. The cap was being gaily passed from hand to hand, and at last was given to Leonardo well filled with pennies. Down leaped Leonardo from the table as lightly as a bird, and went up to Botticelli with a great show of feeling. He took Sandro's two hands, and Sandro tried to draw away. But Leonardo's hands, though as white and slender as a princess's, were as strong as iron—hands so delicate they could paint exquisitely each separate hair in a curl of a portrait, and so full of strength they could bend horseshoes. Sandro could not escape and had perforce to turn up his palms.

"My dear Sandro," said Leonardo, pouring the *denari* into the outstretched palms, "I think there is as much as a *soldo* here; buy yourself with it a piece of the coarsest serge cloth, cut it yourself, and you will have something to cover your shoulders with, and will cease to grieve your good friends by being exposed to the chill evenings of spring."

Before Sandro could think of a sufficiently clever retort, Leonardo had whirled around and was presenting the jerkin to Andrea del Verrocchio.

"My dear Master," said he, "please accept this little offering as a slight token of the great regard this company bears you. May I suggest without vanity, the sketch being my work, that you tack it up on the wall here for us all to view?"

Then, as Verrocchio laughed so hard that tears formed in his eyes, and as the rest of the company held their sides with mirth, Leonardo, who up to this time had preserved the most serious face imaginable, could no longer hold himself in check. His own laugh echoed with the rest.

Perugino and Filippino Lippi together, standing on the table, were tacking up the jerkin for all to see. "Halt! Halt!" cried Sandro, "this has gone far enough! I ask Leonardo's pardon for the time I invited him to dinner and all the food on his side of the table was made of painted clay, and for the time I painted a donkey on his cloak so he would always have a horse to ride!"

"What about the time you feigned to be sick in bed, and

I came and found the covers heaped up, and while I felt in them for your face, you pounced out from under the bed and tried to turn *me* into it?" asked Leonardo laughing.

"Oh, dear Leonardo, I ask your pardon for that, too."

"This new humbleness will be vastly improving to your soul," smiled Leonardo, and to the great amusement of the company, the jerkin remained on the wall. And now Sandro had an opportunity of viewing the picture, and when he saw it, showing himself half clothed and handing out his garments in all directions, and entitled: "Alessandro Botticelli shares his clothes," he too joined in the glee as heartily as the heartiest, and clapping Leonardo on the back exclaimed: "I have met my match at last!"

Needless to say, Filippo and Giovanni had enjoyed this friendly jest as much as anyone. Before the company broke up, Leonardo came to them and talked to them about his horses and his cats, and about birds, and then he said, his beautiful radiant face brighter still with the joy of enthusiasm: "Men, too, shall one day fly through the air. Ah, perhaps it will be given to me to show the way." And then, pushing back his golden hair with his white hand, he took up his lute and improvised softly to it:

> "On strong swift pinions Man shall fly:
>   The miracle shall be at last,
> That Man shall make reality
>   The winged stories of the Past."

The lad looked at him with mingled astonishment, awe, and admiration as he spoke of his plans to invent a machine

HE TOOK UP HIS LUTE AND IMPROVISED SOFTLY TO IT.

on which men could sail through the air like birds. "Truly," said Filippo as they left the studio together, for Giovanni was spending the Easter holidays with him, "your Leonardo da Vinci is everything and more than you have told me. There never was such a man since time began!"

The next day, Holy Saturday, there was so great a crowd gathered in and around the cathedral that it seemed as if all the inhabitants of Florence and the surrounding country must be there—which was in fact almost the case. Filippo and Giovanni had come early with Filippo's cousins, and had secured a good standing place inside the church but near the door. They like everyone else were waiting for the great yearly ceremony of *Il Scoppio del Carro* (The Bursting of the Car), which heralded in Easter. The cost of this ceremony was paid by the powerful Pazzi family, with whose name it was closely associated. An ancestor of theirs, Pazzo dei Pazzi, was supposed to have been the first knight to plant the Christian banner on the walls of Jerusalem in the First Crusade, for which bold deed he had been given some flint stones from the very walls of the Holy Sepulchre itself. These with the deepest joy and reverence he had brought back to Florence, where they had been used in this Easter ceremony ever since. According to one story, he had kindled the sacred fire at the Holy Sepulchre, and in order to keep it alight, had ridden backwards all the way from Jerusalem to his native city.

"My," said little Luca looking up at Filippo, "Messer Pazzi was a wonderful knight if it is true he rode backwards all those days to shelter the Holy Fire against the wind. Do you think he did it the *whole* way, Filippino? Why didn't he make a lantern to keep it burning in?"

"I don't know. Perhaps he did, Luca boy. That reminds me," said Filippo turning to all his cousins, "it was a member of that family, little Virginio Pazzi, that I went swimming with in the Arno the other day."

"You mean that you saved from drowning. It was the bravest, the noblest thing ever!" exclaimed Margherita. Filippo would no doubt have been pleased to see his pretty cousin's look of affectionate pride in him, but he did not catch it at all. He had let the pushing crowd separate him from his cousins a little, and was saying in a very low tone designed for Giovanni's ear alone:

"There is something that Virginio said that troubles me very much. In the excitement of finding you, dear friend, it slipped my mind, but now that I recall it, I must have your advice what to do. Perhaps it is just a child's story—but… Well I'll tell it to you when we are alone."

Shortly after, the solemn High Mass began. The vast interior of the majestic cathedral, with its magnificence and treasures of art, was dominated by the heaped lilies on the altar. The highest clergy of the city, in their richest vestments, officiated. Outside the open door stood the *Carro*, a huge towering structure on wheels, brown in color and painted with dolphins, the emblems of the Pazzi family. It was covered everywhere with an endless array of fireworks, waiting to be set alight, and had been drawn hither by three pairs of milk-white oxen wreathed in flowers. From its top to the high altar of the cathedral stretched a slender wire.

At almost the stroke of mid-day, as the High Mass reached the *Gloria in Excelsis*, the Archbishop of Florence solemnly set alight with fire struck from the sacred flints, a little metal dove. The figure flew by mechanism along the wire until it reached the car. A deafening roar! A blinding light in many colors, in the form of stars and flowers and spiral and circles! The crowd tumbling over one another in eager excitement!

Meanwhile the dove returned of itself to the altar, the *contadini* present gazing at it superstitiously and murmuring: *"La Colombina"* (the dove) "flies crookedly this Easter. Ah, alas, alas; it will be a bad year." But the mass of the crowd was following the car, which, giving forth the thunder of a cannonade and blazing in glory, was taking its way towards the "Canto dei Pazzi," a street-corner near which several of the Pazzi palaces were situated, where the end of the ceremony always took place.

It was nearly evening when the friends at last found themselves alone near Andrea's studio. Filippo had related the whole story of what Virginio had told him he had heard through the keyhole. "You see, there were, according to Virginio," he summed up in conclusion, "many men there—foreigners and others—and they all seem to have echoed Francesco Pazzi's words: 'Lorenzo de' Medici and his brother must be killed.' If it was a jest or merely excited talk, I don't want to be an informer on innocent persons. But if… *Amico mio*, I ask you what I should do?"

"There has not been a political assassination in Florence for years and years. I can't think they mean to commit one."

"Nor I either, as I tell you. Still, if anything *should* happen to Lorenzo and Giuliano, would not I be as much responsible as the assassins themselves?"

"I'll tell you what, Filippino. Look up Virginio and learn from him what has happened since; he seems an expert at listening at cracks!" Giovanni's lips turned up with scorn at the last.

"Dearest Giovanni! That is exactly the thing!"

"Yes, I think so. A little fellow like Virginio may have misunderstood everything; just imagine, for instance, his having heard Leonardo talking yesterday! he would have thought the famous Sandro Botticelli really couldn't afford a doublet."

"Well, I'll pump Virginio for the latest news—if any."

"And let me know the outcome… Ah, look yonder," Giovanni interrupted himself.

Both boys reverently removed their caps. Coming towards them were a number of men robed from head to foot in black, their black head-coverings only leaving space for the eyes to look out. They were bearing a covered litter, and walking in absolute silence, like beings of another world. They were members of the world-famed Compagnia della Misericordia (Company of Mercy), founded some two-hundred-and-forty years before by an humble porter named Pietro Borsi. This Borsi, with an associate, Luca, and the other porters of the city, raised money among themselves and had six stretchers built, with which they answered all calls to move sick and injured persons without cost.

"Oh," exclaimed Giovanni catching Filippo's arm, "see the poor dog!" He pointed to the place where a knot of street-boys had suddenly appeared. In their midst was a shrinking animal that every one of them seemed trying to hit with stick or rock. "Shall we make a sortie?"

"Indeed, yes!"

Neither of them thought of Giovanni's broken wrist. With a determined cry, they swept down upon the thirteen or fourteen youngsters. "Leave that dog alone, you wretches, or—I'" "What's it to you?" "You'll soon see!" The fight was on in earnest, and, whatever the odds, Filippo and Giovanni were not ones to turn back.

Sticks and stones designed for the dog were turned against them, but the two threw themselves so quickly and boldly into close quarters that few of the urchins could use any other weapons than their hands and feet. Giovanni with his crippled arm was at a serious disadvantage. Filippo, catching a sudden glimpse of him hemmed in by foes, flung himself with new fury against his own opponents. He hardly felt their knocks, but his strong finely-trained blows seemed every one to strike home. He won to Giovanni's side, and together they fairly sprang upon the whole circle at once. This way and that, Filippo dashed his fist like lightening, always landing it even as he tried to shelter Giovanni. "It's good it's my left hand that's hurt!" gasped Giovanni as he sent a boy whirling like a top. Another, and another, and another boy dropped to the pavement or took swiftly to his heels. The friends were masters of the field.

"Now for the dog," said Giovanni, his face twisting as he felt of his broken wrist. "Where is it?"

Filippo, wiping away some of the blood flowing into his eyes from a big gash in his forehead, looked about. "Ah, thank Heaven, it's over there by the door."

The boys ran to it. "The poor thing, it's foot is broken," said Filippo. "Do you think we can set it, Gian?"

"I know who can do so better than we—Leonardo."

"We'll take it to him, and when the leg's splintered up, we'll carry it home. Poor dog, you'll have a master in future."

Giovanni pressed his friend's hand. Then as Filippo gently took the dog up, he exclaimed: "Ah, if there could only be a Company of Mercy for animals! Do you think there will be one some day, Filippo?"

"You and I can be one." Filippo raised his hand over the dog's head and pledged himself: "I swear to save all animals from hurt and pain to the full extent of my powers, so help me God."

"And I likewise, so help me God," echoed Giovanni. And each in turn kissed the sacred image that set in a niche in the wall of the house by which they were standing.

The next few days, the dog being comfortably settled at home, Filippo spent all his spare time in watching the Pazzi palaces and in trying to catch sight of Virginio. In the circumstances, he thought it unwise to make a call on him, and hoped instead to meet him casually so that he might ask him questions without danger of being overheard.

The sober days of Lent were over, and Easter had ushered in the happy months of the year, with their many, many holidays. March twenty-fifth, the *festa* of the Annunciation, when lilies filled every shrine of the Virgin in the city, was also the first day of the Florentine new year of 1478. On this day, the third since Easter Sunday, Filippo did come across Virginio. "No," replied the little boy to the anxious query put to him, and looking quite crest-fallen as he confessed it, "I haven't anything else about Lorenzo and Giuliano; perhaps they were all joking when they talked about killing them—and they didn't sound as if they were joking," he added. "But"—he brightened up—"you can come home with me and see the new statue we've got. It's a real Greek antique!"

Filippo excused himself, and sped on to Andrea's studio. "Hurrah!" he greeted Giovanni with. "It's just as you thought—all a child's imagination. The little monkey practically had to admit it."

"Fine! With that off our minds, we can plan some dandy jokes for the Feast of Fools!" (April Fool's Day).

So the days passed for the two friends each happier and merrier than the last. Giovanni was making splendid progress in his art apprenticeship; Filippo, studying as he had never studied before, was going forward in scholarship by leaps and bounds. In no time a month had gone by.

It was Sunday morning, the twenty-sixth of April. Filippo, in Florence, was out alone, for Giovanni was spending a week at some distance from the city.

As he strolled along, lost in thought, he was startled by the sudden approach of a small boy. It was Virginio. "What in the world are you doing, Filippo?" he cried. But then, much more interested in his own news than in where Filippo was going, he burst out with: "Guess what! I ran away from my tutor on purpose to find you and tell you. We are, too, going to kill Lorenzo and Giuliano, just as I told you! I heard it! I heard it!"

A shock ran through Filippo from head to foot. "When? When?"

"Today!" cried little Virginio, jumping about in excitement.

"Oh, it can't be! What did you hear?" demanded Filippo.

"It's a sure thing! I could only hear a little 'cause they talked very low, but everyone was together again, more men than before, and the very last thing Francesco said was: 'Then it's absolutely settled the two shall die to-morrow; good.'"

"Are you *sure*, Virginio?"

"Virginia Pazzi doesn't lie," retorted the little boy in a hurt tone.

"But what else—Surely you heard something else! Where will—it—take place?" Filippo, clenching his hands, could hardly keep from screaming the question.

"I tell you, they spoke low. But he said *today*. Today! Isn't it exciting?"

"Yes," gasped Filippo. "And now I must go, Virginio. I'm late. Good-bye. Good-bye."

Stammering the words, Filippo whirled about and sped down the street as if demons were after him. At the turning, he glanced back. Virginio still stood where he had left him, staring after him in wide-eyed amazement.

His heart beating wildly, Filippo dashed on at full speed until he drew up beside the door of the Medici palace on the Via Larga. As usual, there were several loiterers about. "Are the Magnificents within?" he gasped.

"Where have you been keeping yourself, youngster?" replied one of the idlers scornfully. "Haven't you seen Lorenzo and his guests—a brilliant company, on my word!—making for Il Duomo?"

Hardly had he said the last word than Filippo was flying for the cathedral with all the speed that was in him. The great door was open, and, all dusty and disheveled as he was, and heedless of the throng of worshippers who stared amazedly at his boldness, he started down the nave without so much as bending his knee or crossing himself.

The vast interior of the cathedral, so long and so high, swam about him. The High Altar, near which he knew those whom he sought would be, seemed miles off to his whirling head. The Latin words of the Mass went solemnly on, but he heard not one. Almost staggering, yet moving swiftly, he reached the fenced-in choir. Near it he caught sight of the calm, highly intellectual face of Angelo Poliziano, or Politian, Lorenzo's close friend and the greatest poet and scholar of the Laurentian Age. Then he saw the homely features of Lorenzo himself—actual ruler of Florence, fine poet, dazzling patron of Art and Letters, a power in Europe without any title save that of Florentine citizen.

In a swift rush he had darted through the midst of Lorenzo's companions and stood at his side. "Magnifico!" he cried in a low voice. Several of the men about Lorenzo clapped their hands to their daggers at the surprise, but Il Magnifico, accustomed to mingle familiarly with everyone and hear all petitions, turned good-naturedly and without a shadow of fear or even of astonishment at this approach during the sacrament of Mass. "What is it, my lad?" he asked under his breath.

Filippo, blanched with fear, struggling for breath, gazed about for an instant almost confusedly. How could he tell which were Il Magnifico's friends and which his enemies? "Messere, Messere, they are going to try to kill you!—today! And your brother!" Then, becoming equal to the emergency as he always did, Filippo noted, even as he caught Lorenzo's incredulous smile, several of the faces of the circle grow deathly white.

The Mass droned on. Filippo said nothing further but kept his eyes full on the Magnificent's face. Lorenzo, looking keenly at him, said very softly: "Stay by my side till Mass is over, and before we leave the church, Giuliano and I will hear what you have to tell us."

Filippo, a little color creeping back into his cheeks, bowed his head. Thank God, the brothers would be safe if they stayed here, for surely no man would dare commit murder in the House of God. Moving out from the circle a little, he caught sight of Giuliano on the opposite side of the choir—handsome and kindly, the best-loved of all the Medici. Had Filippo known that Giuliano, who was not well, had been induced to come to church by Francesco Pazzi and another of the conspirators, who made a special trip to fetch him, and had he known that as the three walked up the aisle together, Francesco had put his arm around Giuliano's waist as if in friendship, and found that he wore no cuirass or dagger, Filippo would have known that not even the altar of the cathedral would give safety. He did not know it, and slipped back near Lorenzo.

The Mass bell tinkled—the assassins' time was come. At the same moment, Giuliano and Lorenzo were set upon. Filippo only saw the latter. A knife swooped, but the blow was aimed too high, and Lorenzo dodged. In an instant his own sword was in his hand and his mantle wrapped about his other arm. Filippo with Lorenzo's loyal friends, sprang to protect him.

Filippo was unarmed; his robe was his only shield. All was so sudden that he did what he did instinctively, and for a minute blindly buffeting the assailants, retreating with Lorenzo, leaped the low rail of the choir, ran before the altar, darted through the gate by which the choir boys entered, and found himself in one of the two sacristies. Lorenzo's adherents swung shut the heavy bronze doors, and all at last could look at each other.

Filippo always remembered afterward the moments that followed as a sort of dream. He knew later, he did not know then, that the bodies of Giuliano and a faithful companion were lying dead on the floor of the church. Lorenzo had received a dagger cut on the neck. "The dagger may have been poisoned!" someone said. Filippo touched Lorenzo's arm: "I will suck your wound for you, Magnifico." A youth thrust himself before Filippo, eyeing him suspiciously. "That is my privilege," he cried, and set his lips to the wound.

Some other youths, also suspicious, drew Filippo off to the other side of the room. "Now how do you account for yourself?" they demanded. Looking at them with his proudly honest gaze, he told all from end to end. "Mind," he concluded, "I know no names except those of the guilty Francesco Pazzi and of the innocent father of Virginio, and the fact that many foreigners were involved. Alas," he sighed, dropping his head on his breast, "I am to blame since I did not earlier take warning from Virginio's words."

But the faces of Lorenzo's friends had entirely cleared of their doubt of him.

Now, in answer to shouting and pounding at the thick bronze doors, a youth deeply devoted to Lorenzo climbed up into the organ gallery and looked down into the body of the church. "It is truly our friends!" he called. Those within threw open the doors, and all gathered about Lorenzo and led him homeward, that he might not as yet see his brother's body.

Filippo slipped off by himself. The great bell of the Palazzo Pubblico was still ringing which told good citizens to come together and come armed. The streets were jammed with tumultuous crowds who voiced their adherence to the Medici with screams of "Palle! Palle!", the name for the Medici coat-of-arms with its six *palle* or balls. The populace was shrieking for vengeance on the conspirators.

"There! There!" yelled a giant of a man, waving a knife and pointing at Filippo. "I recognize him! He's a friend of the Pazzi!" Whether the man really had seen him at the Pazzi palace, or only mistook him for someone else, was uncertain. Certain it was that it was no time to argue. Filippo took to his heels and ran for his life.

A part of the mob at once caught up the cry. Filippo, dodging and twisting, fled for the labyrinth of narrow ways and alleys behind Or San Michele, the celebrated church of the guilds or trade associations. At last, hoping he had cast off pursuit, he dared to slip around the church walls so lavishly adorned with statues, and into the dim interior lit by its stained glass windows. The only persons visible were a few kneeling women. Almost spent and terribly shaken by the happenings of the day, Filippo sank down in the dusky corner back of the "miracle of loveliness," the very famous Shrine of the Madonna made by Andrea Orcagna.

He had lain here some moments when a safer refuge occurred to him. "I will ask hospitality of Maestro Bartolommeo; people are too afraid of him to look there." So once again, this time fearful of those without and not of him within, Filippo, having safely gained the Ponte Vecchio, knocked at the door and entered the house of the good old alchemist, his friend.

VIII

The Great Festa

It was five days later, and May Day—a very melancholy May Day with little of the dancing and song and flowers and greenery for which the holiday was famed, for the day before the well-loved Giuliano had had his public funeral. Filippo, at his uncle's, was deep in a beautiful manuscript of Dante's *Commedia*. He was trying to forget the bloody scenes of which he had caught glimpses on that terrible Sunday. The conspiracy had failed, for the people of Florence had risen to the support of the Medici. Many of the conspirators were killed by the enraged population; wholesale executions took place, in which many innocent men, some of whom did not even know of the existence of the plot, met their death. Not only this, but the conspiracy was yet to lead to a long foreign war with its attendant suffering for everybody.

The knocker of the house-door clanged loudly, so that Filippo heard it even in the room where he was. "Ah," he cried gladly, "it is Giovanni returned! How I have longed for him!" He ran to the door himself.

To his surprise, it was a messenger wearing the Medicean device, who met his eyes. "Filippi de' Nerli?" "Yes." "I have the honor then—" and the lad handed him a sealed note with something small wrapped in silk. Breaking the seal, Filippo read the Latin:

"Lorenzo of Florence remembers his new-proven friend and counts himself under debt of gratitude to him."

Then, under the signature, he saw that Lorenzo had added in Tuscan: "Visit me, my boy."

From out the silk dropped a beautifully cut cameo ring!

"I am instructed to tell you," said the messenger, "that Il Magnifico Lorenzo especially looks forward to seeing you in person."

Filippo colored. "To go to Lorenzo would be as if I expected favors," he murmured half under his breath, so that the messenger may or may not have heard. Then he said more loudly: "Be seated if you please, Messere. I shall write my thanks." He walked to a desk, took up a pen, thought an instant, and swiftly composed the following verses in Latin:

> "Magnifico: your gracious words
> Confuse me and amaze
> Since I did nought to merit them
> Or to deserve your praise.
> "Domine jai, my humble pen
> Is dumb before this test:
> Your cameo ring is on my hand;
> Your letter, on my breast.
> "This ring upon my hand, Master.
> Will pledge my hand to thee
> If ever you should deign to find
> You have some need of me.
> "This letter on my heart, Master,

Is not needed to prove
My deep devotion to that
Man I also dare to love."

Then, like Lorenzo, he attached a nota addendum in Tuscan: "Magnificent and Most Illustrious Lorenzo, I beg to sign myself your eternally faithful and humble servitor, Filippo de' Nerli." And having thus gracefully acquitted himself of his thanks in the space of a moment or two, Filippo pressed the missive with the family seal, and handed it to the messenger.

It was mid-summer. The warm days, in other years so joyous, wore something of a sober cast. The cloud of gloom was growing darker over Florence. But the people were to have a day of glorious entertainment nonetheless. The festival of San Giovanni Battista (St. John the Baptist), properly falling on June 24, was to be celebrated with all its accustomed splendor on July 5. And the festa of San Giovanni, the patron saint of Florence, was always the greatest, gayest, most lavish, and most magnificent holiday (with the possible exception of Carnival week before Lent) of all the merry year.

So the great day came, and was welcomed in at eight o'clock of the preceding evening, when the new day began for the Florentines, with bonfires and fireworks, with bells and music, with dancing in the market squares, with feasting and merrymaking, and with a splendid procession that seemed fairyland made real, lit by torches and enormous carved and painted tapers. It was a marvellous and magical pageant of color and movement. There were living representations of spirits seemingly floating in clouds of cloth; of little demons who created great fun by darting out at the crowds and trying to prick whomever they could with their pitchforks. There were men masked and mounted on invisible stilts so as to seem very tall, and dressed like different saints; beautifully or grotesquely decorated cars drawn by oxen or horses, and much else.

With morning, the space between the church of San Giovanni and the cathedral was seen to be roofed in at a great height with blue cloth embroidered with golden lilies. Everywhere were flowers, banners, and rich hangings. At nearly every downtown corner were stands erected by jugglers and street-singers, story-tellers and mock-magicians, and other popular amusers of the crowds. Everyone was in brightest clothes, or was leaning from the windows that faced on the route that the grand procession of the day would take.

Hanging over the railing of a second-story *loggia* or arcade, were Filippo and Giovanni, arms entwined, amid a merry company of artists and friends. "Here they come! Huzza!" Caps and streamers, handkerchiefs and roses waved in the air as in a great burst of trumpets and fifes the head of the train came into view.

In brilliant array the procession moved by to end up at the church of the patron saint. On and on and on it passed, apparently endless; the splendid *carro* that symbolized the Republic; the giant hollow tapers called *ceri* or towers, some of them as tall as a house and mounted on wheels, and whirled about so fast by persons inside as to make one dizzy, and painted and moulded with pictures of all sorts; the representatives and offerings of each of the guilds; the tributes sent by the subject towns and territories of Florence; the gorgeous banners; the distinguished citizens; all notable foreigners in the city, some hailing from countries as far off as England and Spain; the religious depictions, including John the Baptist himself, holding his iron cross; the gaily costumed peasants carrying torches; even the richly caparisoned horses that were to compete in the races in the evening.

"Ah," breathed Giovanni as the last whirling towers were lost to sight, "that was a spectacle to see again!"

After the heat of mid-day was passed, athletic games were held, given in sumptuous costumes and with a wealth of colorful ceremony. Then, when the sun was slanting lower, the reckless horse-race was run for the palio prize, a most magnificent piece of the finest cloth of Florence which had taken skilled craftsmen many weeks to weave. The *festa* of St. John was near its end.

The summer night, loveliest of all hours in the Florentine year, was sweetly scented and magically clear as Filippo and Giovanni strolled together through the streets. All at once Filippo gave a start and exclaimed: "See the maiden up at yonder window! I know her!"

"She is weeping," said Giovanni.

"You have chosen a perfect time to come," said Lorenzo de' Medici, greeting Filippo warmly; "but why did you not come sooner?"

"Pardon me, Magnifico. I hoped it was sufficient to write my profound appreciation of the honor you did me."

"Your verses were charming. But I want those who are devoted to me to be near myself. Remember"—Lorenzo tapped Filippo's arm—"I expect to see you often hereafter. I have been making inquiries about you, and find from that fine old scholar, your master, and from others whom I trust, that you are a rarely gifted lad and will make your mark in literature one of these days. And when that time comes, I hope I shall have made it possible for you to say, 'I owe a little of my fame to Lorenzo.'"

Filippo blushed and dropped his eyes. "Messere, you make it very hard for me to say what I want to say," he stammered.

"Speak on," encouraged Lorenzo.

"Messere, perhaps I can tell you better if I put it as a story. There is here in Florence a very beautiful maiden who for many months has loved a worthy gentleman to whom she is betrothed. The man has been away for a whole year trading in the East, and came back last week to marry the lady."

"Very pretty. What prevents the marriage?"

Filippo hesitated, and looked appealingly at Lorenzo. "Magnifico, the man bears the name of one of those who killed your brother! But Messere," he rushed on, "the man was hundreds and hundreds of miles away when that hideous deed was committed! He knew nothing of it, he is glad to change his name as the Government demands."

"What is the damsel's name?"

"Bianca Roselli, Messere. She is La Bella Bianca (the beautiful Bianca) to me. I found her lost ring for her once, and tonight I saw her weeping at her window. *Domine mi*, will you make it possible for me to serve her again, by telling her the marriage will be allowed?"

"You set my power with the government very high," said Lorenzo with a smile. "Well, I shall look into the case, and it may be, present it to our magnificent Signoriat for consideration. (The Signoria was the highest governing body in Florence.) It seems an exceptional one."

"Thank you! oh, thank you, my Master!"

"And now, in return, you must spend an hour with me, looking at some of my treasures of Art and Learning," smiled Lorenzo, putting his arm across Filippo's shoulders.

"Master, forgive me, excuse me. My dear friend is waiting for me outdoors."

"Ah, you would never make a fortune at a court, lad!" cried Lorenzo, laughing heartily. "Methinks I will love your friend as well as I do yourself. Hie, Matteo, look up the boy waiting outside, and bid him come in."

And in this manner Filippo and Giovanni came to be honored guests not only of Lorenzo the Magnificent, but also at La Bella Bianca's wedding.

The year and a half of war and suffering had gone by, and several years of peace and prosperity after it. Filippo and Giovanni were no longer boys, but youths of splendid talent. Giovanni's name was on people's lips as a young painter of glorious promise; he had just been admitted to the painters' guild, proving that he was a tried and tested artist and no longer an apprentice to art. Filippo had in this same week won his first trophy in a knightly tournament, where he had ridden and tilted with great credit to himself. But he was prouder far of the honor that had been awarded him today. In a magnificent poetical contest, with the famous poets Angelo Poliziano and Lorenzo de' Medici as judges, he had won the supreme prize, a wreath of laurel carved in silver. His old teacher, Messer Cosimo, had embraced him with tears of joy; Giovanni had kissed him on both cheeks.

"And what," asked Lorenzo afterwards, "can I give you in celebration of your triumph?"

Filippo, who had long ago become a much-loved member of Lorenzo's world-renowned group of brilliant youths and men, smiled back at his patron. "You know I want nothing except your continued favor to those dear to me; Giovanni, my old teacher—"

"*Per Bacco!* you are the worst of favor-seekers," cried Lorenzo, laughing at his jest; "you always ask for others and not for yourself—so that it is downright impossible to refuse you!"

That afternoon, Filippo and Giovanni ascended the steep path up the beautiful hill of San Miniato which overlooks Florence from the south. They carried over their arms and in their hands as many bird cages as they could bear. When they reached the height near the famous Church of St. Miniatus and their eyes rested on the City of Flowers far below, they began to open the doors and let out the little wild songsters, larks and nightingales and other birds that had been born under the open sky and cruelly caught. Their gaze followed the birds as they first timidly fluttered and then soared away to freedom.

"I would that we could make all living things as happy as these birds," said Filippo.

"As happy as we," said Giovanni.

"As happy as we."

"In our friendship," added Giovanni.

"In our friendship."

And because at that time youths and men did not hide their feelings, the two handsome youths, the dark haired and the light, stood with arms entwined and hands clasping upon the hill.